OTHER TITLES
· FROM ·
SERPENT'S TAIL

M A S K S

FORTIES' *·CHILD·*

FORTIES' *·CHILD·*

Tom Wakefield

SERPENT'S
TAIL

BRITISH LIBRARY CATALOGUING IN PUBLICATION DATA

Wakefield, Tom
Forties' child.
1. Coal miners——England——Midlands
2. Midlands (England)——Social life and customs
I. Title
942.4084'092'4   DA670.M64

ISBN 1-85242-116-9

First published in 1980 by Routledge & Kegan Paul Ltd.
Copyright © 1980 by Tom Wakefield

This edition first published 1988 by
Serpent's Tail, 27 Montpelier Grove, London NW5

Printed in Great Britain by
WBC Print (Bristol) Ltd.

For my father

Contents

On the mountain, stands a lady,
Who she is, I do not know.
All she wants is gold and silver,
All she wants is a nice young man.

So come in my Rosie dear,
Rosie dear,
So come in my Rosie dear,
And I'll go out to play.

Skipping rhyme

I

The Cock Pheasant

I first got to know my father by accident, or perhaps, by two accidents. His and mine. I am not talking about conception. Unlike many people I have little recollection of early childhood. I remember no mother bending over me, no mother telling me stories, no mother cuddling, comforting me or punishing me. My mother was there and she must have cleaned, clothed and provided meals for me. Up to the age of five, my memory is either blank or indifferent as to her presence. My father left for work before I was awake and returned blackened with pit-grime in the late evening. He worked and provided. I do not remember him doing or representing much else. The accident changed all that.

The year was 1940, I had just started school. At five years of age I saw less of my parents than before. I left for school each day with a tin containing a gas mask and some sandwiches for my morning break. My mother was now part of the war effort and worked 'nights' in a factory thirty miles from our home. She and other women like her were collected in a coach and delivered to a munitions factory for the night. They were delivered back to us the next morning. In the meantime, I caught glimpses of a woman who either slept on the sofa with her teeth in a glass nearby or a woman who was too fraught and exhausted to talk much.

Sometimes, usually of a Saturday night, I could hear my parents' bed creaking; sometimes I heard a sigh. I never knew what this mystery was all about, but at least it did let me know they communicated. I used to think they were plotting and talking secrets through the paper-thin walls. I believe that if I had known they were making love even at that relatively early age I might have been more kindly disposed towards both of them — even as a child if I had known that I had probably emerged from one such Saturday night session I might have felt less apart from the two grown-ups whom I called 'mam and dad'.

Then one day my dad wasn't there. I did not ask what had happened but was pleased to hear three days later that I could come home at lunch times from school because my dad would be there. It was strange to see him, clean and dressed in his suit and white silk scarf. His right arm should have shocked me or at least have aroused some curiosity. I didn't ask him about it but it was impossible to ignore it completely. It stuck out from him as though it had been erected on some piece of weird scaffolding; wood, wires and plaster of Paris held it in a permanent half salute. Only the fingers jutted out into the air. These too might just as well have been covered because they did not move.

He walked about a good deal, the end of the school summer holidays were partly to blame and economically there was little else my father could do. Fortunately, he had never smoked and a pint of bitter on a Friday and Saturday were the limits of his strained resources. He talked to me as though I were an adult. I liked this; but perhaps it did help to form the basis of a self-precociousness in me of which I have still not managed to rid myself.

'This row of houses is the best part of Cecil Street. All

2

good workers,' he said as we stood in the communal back-yard of the houses in front of us. Our house was one of them but his evaluations were usually truthful. In each house there were two rooms upstairs and two down. A back kitchen was attached, and beyond this stood an outside lavatory and a coalhouse. The bathroom was an aluminium tin bath which hung from the back kitchen door. We bathed on Mondays because that was wash day and the open boiler served a dual purpose. In this sense even our cleanliness was restrained by economics.

Each house had a huge stretch of garden. Householders had been requested to 'dig for victory' and the particular row in Cecil Street had done just that. 'You can play in the backyard, but keep off the gardens.' This was law to all the children in the six houses; if they ventured near the gardens they trod down each path with the care of tight-rope walkers. A footprint on cultivated soil, whether it was your garden or anyone else's in the row, meant a heavy sanction. Potatoes, peas, beans and cabbages were tended like orchids; no child ever picked a blackcurrant or gooseberry — it would have been worse than theft. Territorial rights were strictly adhered to. At this time there were no flowers save for the periods when the vegetable plants or currant bushes came into bloom. At the bottom of our garden, my father still clung on to a bit of self-indulgence: a pigeon pen housed twenty pigeons which flew and mated at his behest.

'Keep out of your mother's way and she can get some sleep'; we walked for miles every day, he would usually announce the itinerary in the morning before we left. 'We'll call on Charlie Seager' (he kept pigeons too) 'then go up Huntington Terrace, we might have a look at the German Cemetery and then I'll show you Tackaroo.'

Tackaroo sounded strange and beguiling and I imagined that there might be things like waterfalls, indians and gypsies there. So, as was our custom, I hung on his free arm and trotted along beside him.

3

'No, that's not coal. It's not a mountain. That's slag. Waste. No, those people aren't working on it, they're looking for bits of things to burn.' He answered my questions in staccato fashion. I had overcome the initial shock of finding out that 'Tackaroo' was in fact a coal mine. He brought it to life for me and there was both affection and affiliation in his odd way of answering my already precocious, child-like sense of wonder. I believe I enacted some of my enchantment because I was with him and this was new. I wanted his approval, so my motives for pondering and staring at the *objets d'art* of mining were mixed.

The high chimney-stack was self-explanatory; after the initial gazing I chose not to look at the huge brick tower. For the more I looked the more convinced I was that it was moving, falling against the sky. It was better to look elsewhere. He directed me. Was he conscious of my fears? Perhaps he always had been. I will never know. He would accept them, but not discuss them. His thoughts and words were or seemed totally spare, economic. Even now, I have never heard him speak ill of anyone or say anything alien about a living soul. I have never heard him swear. He has never attended church except for funerals, christenings or burials.

'That there,' he pointed to a curious construction made up of iron girders latticed together to form a tower. This was topped by a platform with further lattice work which encased two huge iron wheels.

'That there is for winding the men up and down. You see the wheels are turning now. That means that the afternoon shift is coming up.'

'Coming up?'

'Ah yes, they've been down beneath us, miles beneath us, and they've been walking where we are standing. They've been at the pit-bottom and the cage is pulling them back up.'

Now it wasn't necessary to feign interest.

'Can I go down dad?'

'No. No. Never if I can help it.' This seemed all at odds to me if he liked it, and he obviously did. Why couldn't I? It was as though he were part of a secret society or fraternity which he feared and loved but clearly he wished me, his younger son, to have no part of. Perhaps his insights were more clear than I could give him credit for and even at this early age he may have detected that my mechanical or physical aptitudes were potentially slender.

'See the tubs,' he pointed with his one free arm and changed the subject all in one process. I wanted to look for the cage but obeyed him.

'There they are, see them. Watch them tip the coal when they come to the end of the track.' The little miniature railway discharged its cargo as he said it would and the empty iron carriages were back-tracked on to another line. The supply of full tubs continued to chunter relentlessly from the bowels of the outbuildings and two men supervised any kind of hindrance to this routine and ritual of the delivery of goods.

'They are working on the "bank", old miners they are.' He was referring to the men. Was that the fate of old miners? Was it good or bad to be working on the 'bank'? It was no use asking my father such questions.

'What do they burn the wood for dad?' He laughed.

'They don't burn it our Tom.' I loved the phrase 'Our Tom' — I still do. However, he only explained things in his own time, so I watched the tubs and the whirring cage wheels until he chose to continue.

'At one time, the Chase must have been covered with trees. I mean real trees.' I was puzzled as the area was dense with forestry. Great pyramids and pagodas of logs were stacked in perfect symmetry before my eyes. If these weren't real trees, what were they?

'It was when they found coal that they began the pine plantations. All these are pit-props; they are from the pine forests.'

'They are trees then, dad.'

'Nothing grows underneath pine,' he said. He could not or would not accept them as trees.

'They use the props to hold up the roof of the pit, as they go along they have to keep putting up the props.'

'Does the roof fall down then?'

'Ah, sometimes, it does. And then men get hurt.'

'There's the cage,' I shouted as it came into view.

'Time to go back,' he said. 'Your mam won't want your dinner to get cold.' I wanted to stay longer but trailed behind him. We passed an enormous manure heap.

'Pooh, pooh' — I held my nose.

'It's good for the gardens, I doubt if we'll have the ponies with us much longer.'

'Ponies?'

'Come on, our Tom. Talk, talk, talk, you'll talk my head off.'

On Sundays I wore my best suit and went to the Baptist Sunday school. I attended voluntarily with no coercion from my parents. I liked the stories, I liked the singing, and they gave you a star for attending and if there were enough stars you received a book as a prize. I went in the morning and in the afternoon. My parents never asked me any questions as to belief or faith. My father showed his approval in a typical fashion.

'Has the man who plays the organ talked to you?'

The organist had said, 'Are you Dick Wakefield's lad?'

'Yes,' I said.

'That's Jeavon Burton, works at the pit office. Good man, Jeavon,' and that was that. I continued attending church into mid-adolescence. As I said, I liked the stories and enjoyed the singing.

Sunday evenings (for my parents) were usually spent at the working men's club, so I was surprised when my father suggested a walk on the Chase. I would have gone anywhere with him.

'We'll get out of your mam's road for a bit,' he had said. He often used this phrase. He couldn't pick the bilberries very easily and I was having to do most of the work whilst he held the tin. Perhaps my fatigue or boredom from kneeling and picking the dark blue berries gave me the impetus to make my enquiry.

'How did you do it?'

'What?' he asked, as though his injured arm were on another planet.

'Your arm.' I held the tin and he explained it to me. I don't think I understood the details but the suffering was conveyed.

A wall of coal-face had collapsed near him. Part of it had pushed him forward towards the tension end of the conveyor belt. In order not to get mangled up in the rollers he had held his arms forward as protection. The right arm had got caught up in the machinery and saved his body. The only way to get him out was to reverse the gear-head whilst his arm was still entwined in it. It was broken, fearfully lacerated and the nerves damaged. Hearing this from him as a child drew me to him; he never cuddled me, but I wanted to cuddle him, look after him. Instead I picked the bilberries much faster and filled the tin. It was good fruit. Cannock fruit, and what was most important, it was free. Bilberry pie was never scorned but I remember complaining about other food and receiving suitable admonition.

I stared at the plate of onions in 'Bisto' before me. This was our meal together with a slice of bread.

'I don't want it. I'm fed up with it,' I said.

My mother was outraged and shrieked at me. This made matters worse and I sat immobile and sulked.

'Speak to him,' she ordered my father.

'Eat it,' he said.

I did as I was told.

During this period my father was on 'box' money for ten months. This amounted to £2 per week and all of our family of four had to live on it. Apart from the 'Bisto' and onions my parents absorbed alone our poverty-stricken state, denying themselves any leisure that might cost a single penny.

This particular period (although difficult for them) was joyous for me, because it meant that I could be with my dad. For the first few weeks it was only during the early evening and on the weekends. Fortunately, five weeks after my father's accident I managed to break my leg.

I believe children still play the game. In our row of houses, in our back yard, the children at this time called it 'Darers' — whoever dared to do the most dangerous thing became the leader of the group — if you failed on three consecutive dares you were excluded. I was never a leader but usually managed to scrape along with the group without being kicked out.

After three or four rather mediocre 'dares' our leader stunned us into silence by attempting and achieving one of incredible magnitude. A totter's cart had been up-ended in the yard. Bereft of a horse, it rested on its shafts presenting a steep wooden platform that was the base of the cart at an angle which rose to the sky. The back of the cart was approximately three or four feet high. With great speed Jimmy ran up the sloping platform and jumped over the back-flap of the cart onto the ground below. Someone else managed it, but only just.

'Your turn.' I knew I wouldn't achieve it, but if one tried less self-esteem was lost.

I remember my foot hitting the back-flap. And like some poor untrained horse in an impossible steeplechase I crashed to the ground. The horror was immediate. My leg sent agonising darts of pain throughout my body. I could not move. I cried. The rest of the group might have thought that they were being helpful. They carried me in the most fearful fashion to our back door. This transportation only increased my anguish and my parents were greeted at the door by my agonised screams.

I was placed on the sofa. The doctor was sent for and

arrived at about seven in the evening. Retrospectively what happened next almost seems like the scene from a Western film. The doctor ordered my father to get some wood, he came back with some strips that had been wrenched from his pigeon pen. These make-do splints were strapped either side of my twisted leg. An ambulance was ordered for the next morning. The doctor left. I think I must have cried and whimpered all through the night. If I slept, it was fitful. I remember that my father sat at my side all through that night and at intervals he repeated

'You'll be all right old soldier. You'll be all right old soldier.'

I was taken to Stafford Hospital the next day. Stafford was nine miles away — an enormous distance for me. I was hospitalised for a fortnight — my father visited every day. The family (through no fault of their own) had more expenses which had to be met. My mother did not, could not, stop working. I was dismissed from hospital with my right leg encased in plaster of Paris. I could walk, but it was a heavy weight to lump about. My father found an old push chair and that is how the two of us were to be seen for at least three months. There was me hopping in and out of a rickety old push chair with my leg huge and white, encased in plaster. And him, with one arm immobilised by plaster, wood and wires. We attended the hospital together. It's my belief that our mutual suffering helped our recovery; if not, then it did make an indelible imprint on to my mind as to us belonging to each other. From this time I had no cause to be puzzled as to what kith and kin was all about.

The walks continued — it is still bewildering to me how my father managed to lug me about — he usually pulled the push chair as it was more easily controlled that way with one arm. There were many visits, but one strange one seemed to be out of place.

In a pine grove, deep in the Chase-land, my father stopped the push chair and I got out. We hopped down a small pathway and there in this open stretch of land were what seemed to be mile after mile of gravestones. It wasn't like an ordinary cemetery — all the gravestones were the same. No crosses, no stone urns, no stone opened bibles, no angels pointing to the sky. Just small gravestones in perfect order, serried in ranks, mile after mile of them. There was just a number on some of the stones. There were no flowers.

'It's the German Cemetery,' he said.

We were at war and were being told daily to hate Germans, after all, we didn't have much alternative. As far as children were concerned all 'Gerries' were bad. The films we saw told us so.

'Have we killed all these dad?'

'Not in this war. The last one,' he said.

'You wouldn't think there would be any more left.' I scanned the gravestones.

'Ah, there are more of them. That's why Uncle Billy, Uncle Charlie, Uncle Johnny and Uncle George are fighting in the Forces.'

'Are they fighting?'

'They must be — they must be somewhere our Tom.'

'Will we win?' I asked.

'Yes,' he said.

When we had returned to the edge of the pine grove we looked back over the rows of graves. He turned to me and his face, which rarely held much expression, was stricken.

'Some of those men,' he pointed to the gravestones.

'Some of those men must have been miners.' This saddened him, and at the time I could not understand why.

For him a miner was a miner wherever they were from and although at the time it was heresy to grieve for a dead German, my father grieved in his own private and particular way, for men of a different generation, for men who were at war with his country, for men who were miners.

A large, brightly coloured bird flew up before us and made a strange strangled cry.

'That's a cock pheasant,' he said.

'Jump in the push chair, your plaster comes off next week and you'll soon be back at school.'

He prepared me for a drawing to an end of an unstated idyll.

'See, there he goes,' he pointed to the pheasant who shrieked as he flew by the hedgerow.

2

Potatoes and Runner Beans

'You're to stay in the back yard, you're not to go down the garden.' The woman, my mother, stabbed at sacking with a sharpened wooden peg and added another piece of cloth towards another rug. It seemed we had enough rugs but her hands were busy. She liked to have her hands busy. When the rug was complete I knew that she would start knitting. She did not look up at me but continued to stab, stab, stab. The back yard was ten foot square, not much space for a seven-year-old.

'I'll have nobody to talk to.'

'Talk to yourself, talk to the dog.' She did not raise her bowed head. She gave me the options, she had heard me doing both on numerous occasions when I was feeling sorry for myself. I left her with the rug. The dog's lead trailed on the concrete floor outside. The collar looped round at the end. I spent five minutes thinking about cowboys and lassos.

'Gunner, Gunner,' I poked my head inside his kennel. I could smell him; cocker spaniels always have a strong smell. At least ours did. He wasn't there, so I crawled inside his home for comfort. It was dark and cramped. I hunched back as far as I could. If I were a dog, I'd bite her bloody ankle. Just as she came out to hang the washing I'd dart out and bite her. The smell overcame my fantasies and I crawled out for some fresh air.

If I stayed as I was, on my hands and knees, just like the dog, she couldn't see me from the window. I squeezed myself through the hole in the wooden fence, our dog could come and go as he liked. That's why the hole in the fence was left there. The gardens were not fenced, no territorial boundaries were drawn but plots were respected. There were six houses in the row, two bedrooms upstairs, two rooms downstairs and a back kitchen which overlooked the tiny yards. The gardens contradicted the meanness of the houses. They were at least a hundred yards in length and thirty or forty feet in width. A permanent growing testament to the present call for patriotism, each and every one had been dug. Dug for victory; the potatoes, runner beans, peas and other vegetables sprang like machine gun bullets from the earth, no flowers, nothing that could not be eaten was allowed to take up space. No footmarks left the pathways which divided these plots. Our garden was a bit smaller than the others on account of the pigeon pen. It took up some space at the bottom and behind the pen six lavatories had been built. They must have been an afterthought, we had no bath so why should they give us a lav?

It was difficult to raise your eyes from the ground, if you did you might stray, the pathways were narrow. You were not allowed to tread on a garden. I suppose that's why I heard the pigeon pen before I saw it.

I stopped some ten yards from it, there was usually a noise coming from it. Pigeons make funny noises when they are locked in a pen. Often I'd sat underneath the landing platform when they were in there, it was never silent. There was always some slight sound going, just like it is when you stand underneath telegraph wires. The noise never goes away. It was very noisy in the pen, there was a lot of fluttering

13

and noises that I'd never heard before. The birds were upset. A rat, it must be a rat, although my dad had said rats could never get into his pen. That's why it was on stilts. A rat had got in there though, something was going on. I was frightened. If I ran and told my mam, she'd know I had crept out of the yard and I knew she'd cane me for it. The cane was hung behind the coalhouse door. Where was my dad? He should have been home, it was Sunday.

Could I kill a rat on my own? Jimmy Ollingbury had said that they ran up your leg, over your belly, onto your chest and then bit your throat. Hypnotised by fear and indecision I approached the back of the pen. I could touch the woodwork with my fingers. I did, expecting something horrible to break through the woodwork and seize me. Nothing happened, I put my ear to it.

'Come on red-un, no more tippling for you. It'll be over quick,' it was my dad's voice. I'd heard him talk to the red hen before but not like that. 'Ah, ah, oh my Christ,' it was him again. He sounded hurt. No longer frightened but curious, I crawled beneath the pen and climbed on to the landing platform on the other side; the door of the pen was not locked but it was held closed by a stick which had been placed through the hook and eye. The door was about three inches ajar. I tried to look inside but it was too dark and a few birds were fluttering from one perch to another. There was less noise than before. I knew my dad was in there. Again I heard him. All the flutterings had stopped.

'Beauties, beauties, beautie . . . ,' men didn't cry, somebody was crying in our pen, so it couldn't be my dad. He never cried.

I pulled the stick from its hook and eye and opened the door. You always had to open pigeon pen doors gently, slowly, so as not to disturb the birds.

I don't know how long I stared at him. I couldn't move, if I'd have wanted to I couldn't have moved. Like everything else connected with the pen I was still. Only his shoulders moved.

14

Deep grunts seemed to come from his chest where his head was buried. All about his feet were his birds. The blue, white, grey and pink bodies were inert except for an occasional bird that involuntarily twitched or shuddered after death, as though it required one more flight. Even if it were a phantom one. Small traces of down were sticking to his large hands which were speckled with blood. I thought of candy floss at the fun-fair, it stuck to you in just the same way. You always had to lick it off. He grunted again, his shoulders heaved but his head remained bowed. I knew it wasn't candy floss on his hands. Silent, bewildered, I waited. He lifted his head. Tears welled from his eyes and coursed his face. I was shocked, not by the carnage, not by the murder and slaughter, but by his tears. Men did not cry. My dad had never cried.

'Who the bloody hell told you to come down here?' His voice was low and angry. More angry than I'd ever heard it, in fact he was rarely ill tempered let alone angry. He wiped his eyes with the back of a hand. In so doing, he added physical discomfort to himself. The down and tiny feathers attacked his eyes fiercely. He blinked, he shook his head as though this would remove the irritation. He raised his other hand, desperate for some sort of relief. 'It's your bloody fault. I told her not to let you come down here.'

It was necessary to lead him out of the pen, help him off the landing platform. He could barely see his way, his foot hit a dead bird which skidded across the floor and on to the landing platform. Its body now in full view for all to see. No one was there. 'Put that blue hen back in the pen,' he said as I helped him from the platform.

'I'll bury them later, all together. See that we don't tread on Joe Burt's garden.' I obeyed and led him slowly and carefully up the narrow pathway. Progress was slow, it seemed a good time to tell him about the way I had crept out. I was more concerned with my own welfare now than I was for the dead pigeons. Perhaps the thought of my mam and some

15

whacks of the cane from her centred my thoughts on the preservation of the living.

'I crept out dad. She told me to stay in the back yard. I crept out.'

'All these vegetables are doing well. It's a good year.' Had he heard me?

'I crept out dad.'

'Ah, they're doing very well. It's no good thinking of space for pigeons when yer need a bit of soil. I can get ten rows of potatoes in that space. Pigeons take a lot of feeding, a lot of care. No time for it, no space, they had to go. There's a war on.'

He didn't seem to be talking to me and I couldn't see what the pigeons had to do with the war. We were approaching the house, I was getting nervous, afraid of my reception.

I tugged his arm, so that he stopped walking for a moment.

'Dad, I told you, I-I-I crept out . . .' I had begun to cry.

'Stop that snivelling. I won't tell yer mam. I'll say I called yer.' He paused. 'I'll say I called yer to help me do what I had to do.'

I was relieved, we entered the house and he ran cold water over his hands. He called out to my mother and informed her that it was 'all done', 'all over.'

'Our Tom helped me,' he called as he dabbed the cold wet flannel across his smarting, reddened eyes.

'Did he?' she made no other remarks but I'm sure that she disbelieved him.

The rug was at an awkward stage and she couldn't lay it down.

'Dad, dad, I won't tell anybody that I saw you crying.'

'You didn't,' he said. 'It was feathers, feathers. It was just the feathers that had got in me eyes. Go and call in the dog. It's time he had some snap.'

'Here Gunner, here Gunner,' I shouted for the dog. I heard him bark. I heard him very clearly, just in the same way that I had heard my dad tell two big lies in less than a minute.

For some reason when I fastened the dog to his chain, I felt a lot older than I was before I had crept from the backyard. I clicked the gate shut and peered over the fence at the gardens. The vegetables were growing but I couldn't see them moving. Not like I could the pigeons. I suppose we could have eaten the birds but my dad buried them later that afternoon. And since then, I've never heard him mention them.

3

The Shelter

The building had taken a day to construct. It looked like an ark, it had no windows, one door, and at the far end wall a piece of iron protruded from the brickwork. The roof was a slab of concrete and so was the floor.

'It's fuckin' useless. Useless, fuckin' useless. You couldn't swing a cat round in it. There's twenty-six men and women and kids in this row. If the raids do get close; and they will. And if we are all supposed to get into this, we'll have to be on top of one another or climb on each other's shoulders. It's worse than the coal face at fives' pit. Fuckin' useless f . . .' one of the men nodded his head at Jack Birch and indicated that the women and children of the row of houses were standing near, as their menfolk viewed the protection offered from air-raids. The bombs had been getting closer, we had heard them in the night. Jack Birch's assumptions were correct but this was no place for swearing. I'd never heard him swear before; the men had finished their shift and all of them were still grimed. 'Sorry, I'm tired,' Jack said. 'It is useless though. It is.'

It was left to the oldest of the men to break the unpleasant, hopeless, stupid silence. If a small child whimpered, then a mother would smack it. Manny Hayes did not have to make much of an effort to get his audience to listen. He was the only one with an idea. This pleased him, so that he smiled as he raised his hand. Just like Indian Chiefs do in cowboy films.

'Hold on, hold on. Hold on a bit Jack. No need to get het up. 'Cos that ain't much use neither.'

One of the women peered into the shelter. 'What's that iron rod doing sticking out of the wall? You could catch yourself on it in the dark.' She left the entrance and shrugged her shoulders.

'You pull that Queenie, if the shelter's hit and the wall falls in and you're supposed to crawl out.' Jack did not patronise, his tone was flat.

'Bloody 'ell,' was all Queenie could add.

'Things ay as bad as they seem. This bloody thing,' Manny pointed to the shelter, 'is what value they set on us. Nobody says we are to go in it do they? I know, I'd feel safer in me own house, so would me missus. But yo' can't tell me, that men like us who is underground all day can't build a better shelter for this row than that thing. I tell yer what. After you've heard what I 'ave to say. We will bloody use it. As a pig-sty, ready made it is. The row will 'ave a pig in that; a bit of pork and bacon won't come amiss.' He put his hand on Jack Birch's shoulder. 'We'll build our own shelter,' his tone was sympathetic.

'Yer what?' Ada Pritchard, like many of the other wives, had to count every penny. The assorted company waited for the yard elder to speak. He coughed, aware that they were waiting. This affected the immediacy of his idea, he coughed again, overcame his shyness and took the stage. 'Now we all know what's happened to Dick Wakefield's pigeons. We know it had to happen, and we're sorry. We know that he needs the ground for taters. What I'd like to know is, what's he goin' to do with his pen?' The crowd looked towards my father. Talking, let alone oration, had never been easy for him.

'Firewood,' monosyllabic and sad-voiced, he answered. There must have been some sympathy for him but it was not voiced. Some of the women made sad tutting noises but that was all.

'That's a good pen, strong, well built. The ground it stands on is well away from our houses. What if we buried it? Buried it good and deep.' Manny was an intelligent man and like many of his generation had not had the time or opportunity to utilise it. He presented his case slowly, tantalising more questions out of the crowd. The women whispered amongst themselves, they might have been questioning Manny's sanity. Older miners did go 'funny' sometimes and these were difficult days.

'Now Manny, now, now. What do we want to go and bury Dick's pigeon pen for?' Ada Pritchard questioned him slowly, there was a distinct trace of consolation in her voice. As though indeed, she did feel that her neighbour was slightly deranged. He answered her sharply, it was the kind of introduction that he had been waiting for. He had engineered the question as though he were some skilled politician. He raised his right arm, turned and pointed dramatically at the pen.

'That there pen is our shelter. It's four times bigger than this sodding thing they have plonked here. If we bury it deep, put in prop supports, we can make it as safe as a tank. You're not telling me that eight men who work underground can't build a shelter, a safe shelter for our women and kids.' He stopped abruptly and let his raised arm fall to his side. We all looked at the pen.

'What about our potatoes?' my mother was forced to view things economically.

'The rest of us will share,' Ada spoke decisively, there was no challenging her statement. The other women nodded their heads.

'It's ten rows,' said my mother.

'We'll share Esther, we'll see you get your due.' My mother nodded agreement and Ada (who had now finished her contribution) turned to the men.

'When?' she asked.

'Tomorrow, we'll start at five in the morning. Sunday will just 'ave to be like every other day. We'll 'ave it finished by evenin'.' The men did not question Manny's optimism with regard to the potential of their productivity. The cause was good enough.

'I can get some pit props in later tonight.' One of the men spoke quietly. We all knew that this meant theft. Everyone nodded, mouths sealed, minds closed; they were the jury, he had already been found not guilty.

On the following Monday the whole street knew about it. The children of our row might let other children look, but not go near it. From the top of the garden all that was visible was a slight mound of earth. Even this had not been wasted, this earth was deemed fit for lettuce and radishes. At first, the other children accused us of being liars. Vociferous in their denunciation, hoping that we would eventually give in to the loud abuse and take them down the garden pathway to view the entrance. We compromised. It was Mary Barton's idea. As she was a girl, we didn't want to give her much credit for it. However, it settled all the doubts.

Mrs Sugden was old, infirm and humped. Her face was besmirched with a strange roaring red mark which covered her left eye and all its surrounding flesh and extended to the right hand side of her nose. She had been married, but we had never known her husband, she was childless, and she had this mark on her. Unlike the deformed old women in a Grimm's Fairy Tale she was not unpopular. Children went on errands for her, and neighbours would give her a bag of coal from time to time. From her house the entrance to the shelter could be seen. When half the children of the street offered to mend her fence, she received the request with no alarm.

'Of course you can ducks, but I can't give you all something. There's too many of yer.' She let us through and from the broken section in her fence the concealed entrance of the shelter could be seen. We were now esteemed, we hoped for bombs. The other children were silenced. The contract with Mrs Sugden we honoured by patching the fence with broken holly and privet, it was a make-do tapestry of repair that would not last a year. Even we knew this. Mrs Sugden did not complain. She never did even though she was crooked, alone, and had that mark on her. My gran said that Mrs Sugden's husband had been a good-looking man when he was alive. Perhaps she looked different then, or perhaps he liked the way she looked. Funny though, as I've said, she had this mark on her, but when you knew her you didn't seem to notice it much.

We began to use the shelter about once a week. You couldn't not hear the siren's wail. The bombs were a bit of a disappointment, all we could hear was occasional thudding noises. When we trod the garden path we would see the sky lit up in one direction or another, but not near us, not even within a mile of us. Rugs and blankets kept us warm down there beneath the lettuce and radish patch. The grown-ups talked much more than they did when they were above the ground. The women were friendlier to each other and the men played cards. Children were told to be quiet and they were. My mother and Mrs Acton both worked four nights of the week out of seven.

'They're bombing Darlaston, Dick,' Mr Acton said to my dad one night when there were more thuds than usual.

'Ah, they are Sam,' was all my dad said. Sam's wife and my mam were in the factories that the bombs were meant for and that was the sum total of their menfolk's concern. Anxiety was rarely expressed outwardly by these men.

Soon the processions down to the garden shelter lost their adventure. The children (particularly us younger ones) would have stayed in our own beds if we could, it was no longer

22

fun to be woken up, chivvied into some kind of action, and then be half frog-marched, half carried, out of the house. One of those nights was to make such an indelible impression on our minds that nothing which followed could compare with its wonder.

The thuds were incessant; as we approached the shelter the whole sky was a bright orange, the glow from it was all about us. For some reason the inmates of the yard stood at the entrance of the shelter steps. It was usual for us to descend immediately.

'God help them,' said Ada.

'Wolverhampton is it?' Jack Birch shielded his eyes from the glow.

'No, it's further, it's further, it's Coventry.' Manny pronounced and gestured everyone to follow his descent into the shelter. The adults were quieter that night, no cards, no joking. We were told to sleep. Some of us asked if we could go above ground and look. For us, the destruction of the city was a beautiful thing to see from where we had stood. However, no-one left that shelter until dawn and by that time the wonderment was over.

The raids lessened. Within a year our nocturnal trips to the shelter had ceased. The men no longer checked the pit-prop supports. The wooden walls ballooned inwards. It smelt like a ton of mushrooms. Its door became unhinged. Pools of water dotted its floor. The wooden bunks became damp and wet. For the adults it had become obsolete. For us it was an enchanting, unsafe, secret place.

We charged a penny entrance fee for any child who did not live in our row. Different things happened down in the shelter on different days. On a Wednesday from 5 p.m. until 6 p.m. we played doctors and nurses down there. This was the most popular day of all and sometimes we earned as much as 9d. At such times, the shelter (which we converted to the hospital for that period) was full. My eldest cousin — he was very old, twelve I think — was the doctor-in-charge.

23

It was he who always decided what was wrong with whom and what should be looked at. Nobody ever suffered a sprained ankle, and something like an injured finger or wrist was beyond diagnosis. No, all our ailments and troubles stemmed from the belly downwards. Some of the girls had chest complaints; but even they mostly had stomach problems. So, usually, they had to take their knickers off and lift their frocks up when they lay on the bunk. We looked and we touched, it didn't matter if it was a girl or a boy. My cousin said we had to keep the hospital a secret. We did for a time. It was Doreen who spoiled it all. She told her mam about the surgery on a Wednesday. All of us got good hidings and Doreen said she had told on us because we had been dirty. I couldn't understand all this — particularly as Doreen had never missed a Wednesday and she always wanted to be the first to be examined.

From then on, we lost interest in the shelter altogether. Two feet of water covered the floor, and the smell of it became really bad. There was talk of filling it in — but the men, somehow, never got round to doing it. I don't know why, it wouldn't have taken them more than a couple of hours. I like to think now that they were too fond of what it had formerly stood for, it was the only truly co-operative venture that I can recollect. It had served its purpose; it was now useless, defunct, a bit of an eyesore and nasty to the nose. Yet, no effort was made to destroy it; it had even been declared dangerous. Like many dangerous things, it remained but was conveniently forgotten.

My mother drew the curtains in the front room downstairs, also the bedroom curtains that faced out on to the street. Likewise, all the curtains in the row were adjusted, as were all the curtains in the street. At 2.30 in the afternoon front doors were opened and we watched the three black cars move from Manny Hayes's house. Wreaths and flowers were on the biggest of the cars. I could see Manny's coffin through the glass sides of the car. There were handles on the side of the coffin and I wondered what they were for. I didn't dare ask. We watched the cars pass and then closed the door and sat in the back room.

'She'll not get any compo you know,' my father was talking of Manny's wife.

'He was killed in the pit, she's bound to get some compensation.' My mother poured tea for us all. Her face strained; angry. She placed the teapot on the table.

'He was killed in the pit. She's got to have compensation.' Her tone was a demand, as though my father was in some way to blame for what had happened. How could it be my dad's fault? Manny didn't even work at the same pit as him. My father continued almost apologetically, not looking at her or me. This was his way of avoiding a quarrel; if there ever was a quarrel, I would side with the loser. It was always him and he never thanked me for my defence, it probably made matters worse and I was never in any doubt that he loved her more than me.

'Haemorrhage, brain haemorrhage. Pit doctor says it could 'ave happened anywhere. There was no bump or anything on 'is head.'

'Well, there wouldn't have bin if he had his helmet on. He must 'ave got a knock.' My mother was adamant, I couldn't quite understand why. I had not detected a lot of compassion to her thinking.

'No proof, no proof. As I've said, she'll get no compo.' My father was saying no more on the matter. He rose to get some coal in preparation for the morning fire.

'I suppose there'll be a collection. One at the pit, and one in the street and that'll be the end of it.' Economics again — how much? I hated her at these times. He didn't tell her how much he would give, but made it clear that he was going to by saying 'Ah'. He left us then to bring in the coal.

'If it's not one thing, it's another,' she said.

The next morning, or it could have been the same evening, the shelter caved in and collapsed. A small hole, an indentation, was left where it had been. It was strange but quite true, not romantic, not bucolic, that indentation was left. Nobody chose to grow anything on it, sometimes we would lie or hide in it, but not often. Now when I think of the shelter, it's not the air-raids, not the secret, exciting bad games that come to my mind. No, it's Mr Hayes that I think of, and that's odd because he only ever spoke to me once or twice. I suppose he has a gravestone somewhere. Funny, how you remember someone like that, particularly as he was old at the time. I would say at least forty years old, and I suppose we could have done without the shelter anyway.

4

The Other Side
of the Cup

I was more afraid of the masks than the gas — or the thought of the gas. It was all that the first year at school meant, apart from food that I couldn't eat, and a room so crowded and noisy that it sent me into a stupor for most of the day. The gas mask drill was all there was to that reception class, it wasn't at all exciting to have that rubber concertina-like thing hanging down in front of you. When you breathed it was a rubbery smell that drifted into the nostrils. I often thought that I would die from that smell, it always put me off my dinner. No, the gas couldn't have been worse than the masks. We carried them to school each day in tin boxes slung across our shoulders. If you forgot your gas mask, you had to go home and get it. That was the first year of school then, gas masks, dinners that were not nice, and a registration call that took at least half an hour because there were so many children in the class. I can't remember the teacher, it's unlikely that she ever remembered any individual child, and given the numbers of children it is highly creditable that she remained sane.

Everything changed in the second year. There must have

been just as many children in the classroom, but somehow the room seemed bigger than the one we had left. Perhaps it was because everything was in order in that classroom, everything was in its proper place. There were corners for this and corners for that, our desks had our names stuck on them, so we knew our place. So did Miss Craddock. You could never go into that room when she wasn't there. In the mornings she looked just the same as we had left her in the evenings. She was never absent or late for school. Sometimes I wondered if she might have slept there.

Miss Craddock was very tall, one of the tallest women I have ever seen. She wore flat shoes; I don't know what her clothes looked like because I never saw her with any on. That is, I never saw her in a frock, or a pullover and skirt. Two large smocks covered her up; they buttoned down the front. One of them was patterned with blue and white daisies, the other one was of pink-and-white check. I liked the daisies one best; I think she must have done too because she wore it more than the pink-and-white one. She never buttoned them, even the two buttons at the top, but she might have buttoned these up had her neck not been so long. She said herself that she looked like a giraffe, yes she did, when she was showing us pictures of animals. Miss Craddock didn't mind us laughing when she told us this, she laughed herself.

Giraffes are beautiful animals and that is why I fell in love with Miss Craddock. I think that is why, although her eyes were big and blue, her complexion fresh, she always smelled as though she had just got out of the bath, she smelt of clean washing, no scent to her just this clean smell.

How would you know what a teacher smelled like? Well, at some time during the day Miss Craddock would cuddle us. Hold us quite close to her and say something very special. We all got the same treatment. As I had never had it at home I suppose I appreciated it more than some of the others. The room was never noisy like the other one had been, this was funny because I can't ever remember Miss Craddock shouting. There were eight groups for reading lessons and she would float from group to group. I can't remember how she taught us to read, in fact I can't remember not being able to read. I had not been in her class long before she extracted me from the groups altogether, she would give me a book that she had brought from home or borrowed from her friend Miss Moore and tell me to read it on my own. Later, she would ask me what the book was about.

'Well now, Tommy, and what do I start you on next, we can't have you standing still, can we?' I didn't know who the other person was when she said 'we' because she hadn't married. I had mentioned to my dad that I'd like to marry her.

'Ah, and you could do a lot worse,' was his reply. I never asked her, I couldn't, although I would have liked her arms around me much more than my daily ration.

Even playtimes were different in Miss Craddock's class. Other teachers disappeared down the corridor into a small room, but Miss Craddock always sat behind her desk. She would send one of us for her morning hot milky drink. This was an honour and we all sat up and looked at her appealingly, hoping that she would choose us to do her a favour. Most of the class went out to play like the rest of the school, but if you wanted to stay inside you could, and if any child had a cold or Miss Craddock thought that they were not well, she would have them in the room with her. I rarely went out to play. I read, sometimes I just talked to her when there weren't too many children in. She was interested in everything and I never had met anyone who could listen as well as she could. Not that I thought she was perfect. No, she told lies, I think they were lies although she never went red when she told them, so for her perhaps they weren't lies at all.

There were one or two scruffy children in our class, but the scruffiest of all was Lilly Minton. She had lots of brothers

29

and sisters and they were scruffy too, they were always having to go to the clinic because they had bugs in their heads. Nobody liked any of them much, least of all Lilly. She was cross-eyed, she had a snotty nose which she wiped on her sleeve, and she smelled really bad. The other children used to call her 'piddle-drawers.' Nobody wanted to sit near her, yet her desk was the closest of all to Miss Craddock. Perhaps she couldn't smell Lilly, she never mentioned it and neither did we if Miss Craddock were near. This is where the lies came in.

There were only three of us in the room, Miss Craddock, me, and Lilly Minton. The others were out at play. Lilly began to blubber and cry, she had a cold and the crying made her snotty nose run more than usual. She kept wiping her face and the snot was all over her. It made me feel sick just looking at her. Miss Craddock took her up, picked her up and sat her on her knee. She wiped her face. Lilly blubbered.

'They're all calling me piss-knickers, boss-eyed, and smelly and . . . . '

Miss Craddock held Lilly to her, just like women did with little babies, she even stroked her hair, yes, that nit-bugger-lugged hair. We all knew it was.

'Lilly, my little sweet. You are beautiful darling. Really, a beautiful little girl, and I wouldn't say that if I didn't mean it, would I?' Miss Craddock crooned. I couldn't believe my ears. I stopped pretending to read, left my desk and stood within a yard of the two of them. Lilly did not look up from Miss Craddock's face. I stared at Miss Craddock; in my childish way I was challenging her integrity. She stared back at me and continued stroking Lilly's head.

'You finished your book Tommy?' she asked.

I nodded waiting for an explanation of what she had said about Lilly. I was jealous. How could she like snotty Lilly more than me?

'I've forgotten my morning drink. Would you go and

fetch it for me dear?' she directed me away from her.

When I returned with the mug of warm, sweetened milk, Lilly was standing near Miss Craddock's side. Miss Craddock had an arm around her, but Lilly's face was clean, her hair looked a bit better, there was no snot around her nose. She had stopped crying but she was still cross-eyed. I placed the mug of milk on the desk and stood at the other side of Miss Craddock. Contrite, hurt, I felt it better for me to share Miss Craddock with horrible Lilly Minton than not have Miss Craddock at all. I watched her take slow sips at the milk and saw it go down the long neck as she refreshed herself with each tiny gulp. Then the shock came.

'We'll share it.' Miss Craddock was referring to the milk.

'Lilly, you can drink from this side. Tommy you can drink from the other side and I'll drink from the middle. It's nice to share, but you have to do it properly.'

Lilly took the first sip, Miss Craddock the second. Now it was her turn to challenge; she handed me the cup, I sipped. Between us we drained the contents just before the bell sounded to let us know that play time was over. Lilly took the empty mug back.

After that I never joined in with the others when they teased Lilly. Sometimes I even sat next to her and listened to her read. If we were making up plays I even had her in my group and gave her parts of a princess or a good fairy lady. Lilly's clothes got better whilst she was with Miss Craddock, her nose stopped getting snotty and she began to smile. There wasn't much point in teasing her any more. Really apart from her eyes, you couldn't say much that was horrible and true. We forgot about her eyes. I suppose Miss Craddock made us all a bit older — or something like that. It's not the sort of thing that you would expect from a lady giraffe, is it?

Miss Craddock stayed at that school all her life. I wonder if she ever changed her room for another one. She never married. You would think she might have done with so many people being in love with her. But then, I suppose she had to spread it about a bit. Her love, I mean.

5

Great Gran

There was no reason why she should choose me to stay with her. I never had any long-term notice of the event. Usually the day before my father would just say, 'Your Great Granny Silvers wants you to stay with her for the weekend.' I was always glad to hear of it, nobody quite understood why she wanted me with her. She had scores of grandchildren and great-grandchildren from which to choose. My mother said that she picked me because I was 'old-headed'. I didn't understand what she meant. When I came back from these weekends, they would ask me what we had done. 'Nothing,' my reply was always the same. They never questioned me further. It was just as well, as my Great Granny Silvers spent most of her time with me intriguing. Family intrigue, I listened fascinated; she swore — really very bad words. She had milk stout delivered and kept gin in the sideboard cupboard. Innocent, spiteful, wayward, but living so much in the present. Anecdotes of the past were strewn my way, some of them shocking, but I never, never, told on her. I suppose that's why I had the weekends in Dudley.

The row of houses that she lived in was called 'The Dock'.

There was a rumour that she owned them. I never found out whether or not this was true. Again as to her heritage, it had been suggested she was Jewish, but this was never mentioned by her and I've never bothered to find out.

'I went off the rails when I was a young girl Tommy,' she explained what that had entailed. I've kept it to myself, as she asked me to. There were duties to be done when I stayed with her. There was no running water to the houses in the row. Each house shared a wash-house-cum-water-supply with two others. Daily, I filled the aluminium bath full of water. She was against bathing completely, she said you caught the 'flu that way, but she did insist on a 'wipe over' each morning. This was why there was always a bath of water, and buckets of water always available in her kitchen.

She was very small, perhaps the smallest woman I had ever known, black eyes — they seemed black. A face full of lines, a mouth full of her own teeth and short black hair. Not a silver thread amongst it, she did look like one of the women in fairy stories. There was little fantasy attached to her and she treated me as though I were a man of forty or more.

'Now our Tom, I never liked our 'Ria' (short for Maria) 'I liked her least of all of them.' She was referring to my grandmother, her daughter.

'She hit your dad on the head with a hammer. Yes, she did, the cruel bugger. And your dad, Dick, he was the best of her boys. She had a lot of boys, eight or nine. Can't remember them all.'

'My uncles, Gran,' I reeled them off for her.

'Ah, yes, but 'Ria was hard. Not like me. True she was widowed early — but she needn't have bin as hard. As I say duck, I never liked her. Do you go to see her?'

'Yes, sometimes I do.'

'Does she give you anything?'

'No.'

'She's not short, shouldn't waste your time seeing her. Oh, that fucking cat. Give it a swipe, look at her, she's scratching

34

the table cover to bits. Just knock her head. A real bitch that cat is. That's why she's only got one eye. A she-cat couldn't lose an eye if she wasn't a bitch. I don't know why I look after the cowing thing. I've got used to her though. Does your dad swear?'

'No Gran, never. My mam does, she says "bugger" and "bloody".'

'Ah well, yer dad couldn't swear, it's not in him duck. Your mother's not well, not as she was. Bird, her name was before she married him, Esther Bird. She's not well duck, no she's not as she was.' Granny Silvers would shake her head at such times. My mother had never complained of being ill to me, so I never answered Great Gran's charity of outlook. I never understood it then, I do now.

'Of course you know you have an uncle who is "funny".' She had told me this before. 'He's in a home. Has bin all his fuckin' life, I'd never have had him put away if it had been me. He is your uncle; your Uncle Jim. Do they take yer to see him?'

'No Gran.'

'Well, he'll be in that place till he dies, they say he's happy enough. Squitch, how would yer know if he was happy when he hardly ever talks. Never has. Not like you or me sweetheart, we could talk their bloody heads off if we wanted to, couldn't we?'

'Yes Gran.'

'How old do you think I am?'

'Don't know; younger than my other Granny.' She laughed.

'Oh bloody hell, don't tell her that, she's my daughter, sweetheart. Hard girl, always was. Now your Great Aunt Ginny is a better kettle of fish. She's got one eye, like the cat. It beats me how our Ginny lost that eye, I can't remember now. She's a good girl though, always was. Her son has never married yer know. He has his reasons, they're not all to do with Ginny, I can tell you that. But he's good to his mother, good to my Ginny and some thoughts are best left.'

Her eyes were bright and clear, possibly her best and most decorative feature. This contradicted face-value appeal with regard to usefulness. She could no longer see to read, this caused her some degree of irritation as she continued to order inexpensive magazines that were full of love stories. They were kept in an orderly pile, she marked them each week so that she would know which was the latest edition. I would spend a lot of time reading to her.

'I liked that one, put a mark by the story and you can read it again next time you come. You read ever so well our Tommy, yer don't miss out a word, I don't know where yer get it from. Your dad's no scholar. Where did you learn to read like that?'

'School, I think,' at eight years I could not remember having been taught to read. Words came easily to me — but numbers were always difficult. I loved reading aloud to her, I enjoyed her dependency.

'Now, I can tell you before you go on any further, he's goin' to be no good to her. She should have stuck with the quieter one, the one that lived nearer to her. As she's a nurse you'd think she'd have more sense, but girls are like that when they're young, sense don't come into it.' She interjected in this way over each story, as though she had special insight into such matters. She was always right about the outcome of each tale, but then it was almost impossible to be wrong as the romantic endings were always predictable. Sometimes she would ask me to read sections twice.

' "He gripped her shoulders and drew her to him. His strong arms encircled her waist. Mary knew it was wrong but she felt lost. She closed her eyes and felt his lips upon her. Lost, lost, I'm lost she thought as his embrace continued." ' I read it more slowly the second time around.

'Ah, that's what happens if you let yourself get carried away, she wouldn't know whether she was on her arse or her elbow after he'd finished with her. They're like that.'

'Who Gran?'

'Oh, men darlin', men, they have to have their bit of pleasure. Life can't be all work and graft for them. He's a right 'un though . . . . ' She would chuckle and pour herself a glass of milk stout. She would give me lemonade but always tip a bit of her drink into it. I would have preferred the lemonade as it was but she insisted that a shandy would make my hair curl. I believed her.

We always played cards. I had told her that I wasn't good at sums and she said she would teach me about numbers. She did. She taught me to play Pontoon and Cribbage. If anyone called to see her whilst we were playing she would cast a newspaper over the playing cards and switch the radio on. I would pretend to read. We would resume our game after the visitors had left. Two or three times I accused her of cheating.

'Oh, ah, caught me out then did yer,' was all she would say to my accusations. Guilt feelings about anything must have long since passed her by. On these occasions she did not concede the win to me, she just said that we would have to play the game over again. Great Granny Silvers rarely lost at cards. If she did lose a game, she would declare that the playing session was over for the day.

'We'll get undressed down here, I'll bank the fire up with some slack and it'll still be warm when we get up in the morning.' Her lack of embarrassment about undressing before me tore away any shyness that I might have felt myself. In any event, we both dressed for bed looking something like American football players. No underwear was removed, our pyjamas went on over the top of these garments. She was also a great believer in bed socks, thick woollen ones. She always had a spare pair for me and we climbed the short staircase upstairs.

A bed was made up for me in the smaller of the two rooms. This must have been appeasement for enquiring relatives — I never slept in that bed. Great Gran took me into her large double bed; before we climbed into bed, the instructions were always the same.

37

'You have a good piddle first, make yourself have a good piddle, there's nothing worse than waking up in bed and having to get out of bed and wanting to piddle. Men do that when they've been on the beer. Bloody terrible it is our Tommy.' She pulled the huge chamber pot from underneath her bed and, just like you do in the hospital, I gave her a sample. 'Good boy,' she would say and then use the pot herself. Usually, I was in bed before her, after climbing by my side she would settle herself with a sigh.

'Ah, oh, well that's another day gone then darlin'. Wasn't too bad, was it? Yer warm enough? Yes you are, I know you are. I'm always warmer when you stay duck. It's one of the bits of getting old that I hate. I've got used to me eyes getting bad, but I'm buggered if I like sleeping on my own. Never got used to it, no never. A hot water bottle goes cold on yer, you know, useless bloody things. If you've got something alive next to yer, you never get cold. When you're not here, I let that cat get in with me. A bastard that cat is, she gets in this bed like a baby. She waits for me to throw the covers up over her and has her head on the pillow. She's got the cheek of the Devil that cat 'as. Now don't go telling yer dad or your uncles or aunts that I sleep with the cat, or they'll say I'm dirty or going funny or something. Yer don't want yer Gran in a home do you?'

'No Gran.' Could they put you in a home for sleeping with a cat? Of course I never mentioned the cat to anybody. In the meantime she warmed her feet on me, cuddled me, I was always asleep before her. She would talk about people I had never known, first names floated across the darkness. Reuben, Frank, Millie — all meaningless to me. It was like being told an unending story — no beginning to it, no end to it; I always slept well.

'Yer dad's coming for yer at three o'clock this afternoon. It's just on nine o'clock now.' I like to think that the hours were as precious to her as they were to me. Or was she anxious to be with her cat again and have the house to herself? She couldn't cuddle the cat, nobody cuddled me except Great Gran. That's what I liked best about her, she held me very close to her, I got used to her smell, it was a mixture of talcum powder and mothballs. When my father arrived there were no great demonstrative farewells.

'Has he been good?' he would ask.

'Ah, lovely, he's been lovely,' she would say. A pat on the head from her and then, 'I'll see you again our Tommy, ah, I'll see you again . . . . '

The visits grew further apart, then stopped.

'When am I going to see Great Granny Silvers again?' — it was a plea.

'You're too old for going and staying over there now.' My mother said this without any explanation. I didn't feel too old. I was never told of Great Gran's death until years after she had died. This might have been a good thing, because for some strange reason I still think of her as being alive. I wonder if she changed herself into a cat — no, she couldn't do that. She must be dead. I still talk to cats though.

6

Theft

It must have been quite unnerving for them. My parents, I mean. Like an enquiring scavenging animal I took full stock of the household every Saturday night. This was after they had gone out for their two hours at the Working Men's Club. I nosed everywhere, standing on chairs or balancing on window frames to ferret out the contents of high cupboards or the tops of wardrobes. They could keep nothing secret from me. She always knew that I had been on the 'search'. 'He's been at it again,' she would say. I think she had given up any chiding or punishments because nothing seemed to put a stop to this 'scritting about' as they termed it. I wasn't tempted to take anything, I just wanted to know where everything was. Once I found a rubber thing with a tube attached to it. I asked her what it was for — it must have been very secret because I was slapped just for finding it. I never stole, that is, not until I saw the men in the brown baggy uniforms with green patches on them.

'Eye-ties, Eye-ties,' some people would call out at them as they sat in groups behind the high wire fence. Yet for the most part, the prisoners of war were ignored. Women might pause and gossip to one another. On the other side of the fence the Italians sat in groups. It must have been the language they used to one another that first attracted me to the compound. Two or three times a week I would return to hear the strange words that they used to communicate with each other. Their talking was quicker than ours, they used their hands more and they made one another laugh a lot. After a few months I found out that if I walked to the compound immediately after school, I would have the road to myself. The Italians would be having a kind of out-door tea and the road was usually empty but for me.

There was no name to that road. It was an untarmacked gravel track which lay on the outskirts of the village. Neither was there an end to it, the track got narrower until it eventually got to no more than a pathway. The pathway led into a pine-forest and dwindled into a gully less than a yard in width. Either side of the gully grew the pine trees; I never ventured too far down that gully. It was very dark between the pines, even in summer time, and I had no liking for the dark. At the beginning of the road there was a sign. Just like there was for any other street or road. It only had one word on the sign though. The word was 'unadopted'.

They must have got used to me sitting there next to the wire fence at the point where the pines lined themselves like soldiers in serried ranks. If they had wanted to escape, they could have got into the forest, there was no fence to stop them. But then, how would they live? Nothing grew under the pine trees and they stretched from where I sat right to the edge of the sky.

At first I was frightened when he called out to me. It was a strange word, it couldn't have been a bad one because he smiled when he spoke. He wasn't as old as my dad, but he was grown up. He must have been grown up or he couldn't have been a soldier. He wasn't as old as any of my uncles though. I sat and looked at him as he stood behind the fencing. He called out to me again. I didn't take my eyes off him, I didn't answer and I didn't get up and run away. I sat there.

He beckoned to me with his hand, he smiled and spoke his funny words. I didn't know what they meant but I liked the sound of them. As if I were conscious of some kind of trespass or breaking some kind of rule I looked to my right and left. There never was any traffic on that road, I was looking to see if there were any other people about. I crossed it. Inches and the fence separated the two of us. He talked again and smiled but I never spoke. Then he held up the paper aeroplane. I nodded, he smiled. When he threw it, he launched it gently but there must have been power in his wrist. The aeroplane sailed over the fence, I backed on to the other side of the track to catch it. It turned in the air, and then glided back to his side of the fence. He laughed loudly, picked it up and launched it a second time. This time it came to rest near my feet. The aeroplane was beautifully made, much better than any of the ones my friends could make. I knew how to fold the paper but the aeroplanes that I made never glided, they just went up and corkscrewed themselves down. I was a clumsy child, never clever with my hands. I picked up the aeroplane, pleased with it. I must have smiled before I walked away.

'Claudio, Claudio,' he tapped on his chest as he called after me. That was his name, Claudio.

He would always have something; nobody had ever given me presents before — only at Christmas and then they were never a surprise because I always found out where they were hidden before the day arrived. And new shoes or new trousers didn't seem much of a present to me. His were different, I never knew what I would get. There was a fir cone shaped into a hedgehog, a sailing boat made out of a matchbox, and a man carved from a clothes-peg. Claudio was a magician, he could change anything into something that I would want. He used to talk to me but I never knew what he was saying, if he laughed then I did. Sometimes I said his name aloud.

He liked me to do that, so I always said it two or three times. It made him laugh when I said it. It seemed daft to me to laugh at hearing your own name but it was the only word I could say and he never tried to get me to say another one.

My mother was very fair about the sweets. She was fair about all things like that. I think she enjoyed everything being rationed. She would always show me the coupons in the book and explain how many were left. The sweet coupons were always used; there were so few that it was impossible to spend much. She counted every sweet and every square of chocolate. I knew exactly how many I would receive each day. It's impossible to say why I began to pass my meagre sweet ration on to Claudio. We had so few sweets — only a child-saint would ever have shared his or her quota — I was far from canonisation as a child. It was out of character for me — poking the half bar of chocolate and the few boiled sweets through the wire netting. I always ran off after he had received them, for some reason I did not want to know his response to the gift. He was the biggest of secrets — I was even afraid of my own fondness for him. I often imagined that if people knew of our trysts I would be hauled up as a spy and people would spit at me and be horrible to my dad. The visits were a mixture of excitement and consternation.

'Hit him, go on. Give him the strap. Take your belt off to him.' My mother had already whacked me with the cane across my legs and my behind, I hadn't cried. She had found this unpalatable. I hadn't denied taking more than my ration of sweets nor had I repented or said I was sorry. Silent and wilful I had endured her anger. There was no doubt I had earned it; I had stolen all their sweet ration for a fortnight.

'What did you tek um for?' my father asked. He looked and sounded most unhappy. Acrimony of any kind always bit into him. He had just arrived back from work and was still unwashed. I couldn't tell him about Claudio.

'You did tek um?'

I nodded. I would not lie to him. I hoped he would give me a whack or two with his belt. Not from any latent tendencies towards masochism, oh no, it was just that I knew that if he did not punish me, then she would punish him. This would hurt me more than the strap.

'Well, there's no sweets for a month then, and that's that,' he said, his belt remained about his waist.

'Is that all you're gonna do?' She was even more angry.

'Ah,' he said and left to wash himself in the back kitchen.

For the next fortnight she spoke to neither of us, she withdrew all communication except for preparing our meals; these she would plonk on the table. Sometimes he would compliment her, trying to cajole words from her with his good will. It was of no use; I witnessed his punishment, it was my fault and I could do nothing to help him. She even refused to go to the club with him on two consecutive Saturdays. He stayed at home, we all did. She knitted and if he turned the radio on she would switch it off. All this he accepted as I knew he would, he loved her very deeply. Nowadays some people might consider him to have been a weak man. I can't view it that way but then I'm biased, I always will be with regard to him.

When she started talking again, he became happy. Even the thought of Claudio could not tempt me to steal the sweets again. That operation could not be repeated. By the standards of the day, my mother was a heavy smoker, my father never touched a cigarette and sometimes when I wished to be spiteful to her, I would let my revulsion with this habit be known by coughing too loudly when she puffed. My vicious histrionics did not stop her. However, I did cut down her intake, just slightly, she never noticed. I extracted a Woodbine a day from the pack.

When I visited Claudio, I always left him with a few cigarettes in the palm of his hand.

The forest keeper startled me. It might have been his peaked cap or heavy boots, his manner was not unfriendly or hostile.

'Haven't you got a home to go to young fellow?' he asked. His concern was genuine enough, it was late September, we had received three days of drizzle and fine rain, and today the weather had made up its mind. It was raining hard. I was standing near the wire netting. I had waited there for a week or more, there were ten cigarettes in my pocket. Claudio and his friends had not appeared. The war wasn't over. They hadn't shot him because we don't shoot prisoners. I had asked my dad, and he had said no, no never. I could not accept that Claudio would just leave like that . . . . where could he have gone?

'Where do yer live anyway?' I told the forester my address.

'You get back there then, you'll get bloody pneumonia standing around here.' He must have been a perceptive man. I had made no inclination that I was going to move.

'The Eye-ties have gone,' he said.

'Gone?'

'Moved them to Wales to work on gravel pits. They might as well be doing something useful, as there was bugger all for them to do here.'

The forester viewed my grief, sensitive, unquestioning, he placed his hand on my shoulder. 'Now, now, you go on; go off back home. They've gone lad, they won't come back.'

I looked at him. He had liked them too. Should I mention Claudio? I remained mute, stunned, as one is when hurt in love. I turned from him, managed to wave, he waved back.

A trail of cigarettes were left behind me. Cast into small pools of water that had been formed by the holes in the un-adopted road. Objects of love left to drown. I never stole again not ever, after that. And I almost forgot Claudio, but not quite.

A year or two later I was reminded of him again.

'Jack Hollingsworth's been killed,' said my father over his meal.

'When? Who told yer?' my mother asked.

'His wider told Charlie, and he told me. Burned to death. He was burned to death.'

'How do they know that?' she asked.

'He was in the tank corps. Killed by a flame-thrower, roasted in a tank,' he said.

'That's bad,' she said.

'In Sicily, it was. The beginning of the invasion,' he said.

'Where's that dad?' I asked him.

'Part of Italy, Italy; it's somewhere in Italy,' he said.

Barry Hollingsworth, the son of the man who had been killed, was a friend of mine, I knew about his dad, but he didn't know about Claudio. I still played with him, I couldn't tell him about Claudio. But then, I know, I knew then, that Claudio could never have hurt anyone. Unless, that is, other people can make you hurt people you don't know. Even so, Claudio couldn't have used a flame-thrower — he made paper aeroplanes, and hedgehogs, spinning tops and things like that. It's stupid to think that he could . . . . I still think of him sometimes.

7

Beyond Reach

The woodlands and heath land known as Cannock Chase provided us with free fruits of the season. Bilberries and chestnuts were the products and neither were left to rot by the local populace. Of course there were blackberries but they grew everywhere. My father led me to believe that the bilberries and chestnuts were peculiar to our region of the Midlands — he took pride in their existence and never an early Autumn went by without us ferreting through the bracken looking for the blue berries which left purple stains on your fingers. Whole families often took part in this scouring operation and lorries would sometimes park in the roadway, ready to weigh your fruit and pay you a pittance for its receipt. Some people sold their fruit in this way but my father resisted these commercial overtures — all of our bilberries found their way into home-made pies or jam.

The chestnuts were harder to come by and less in number. If you knew of a grove of trees, you kept it secret. The gathering of them was also more complicated. If you waited for the prickly cases to fall then someone had found them before you arrived. It was necessary to time things and arrive just when they were about to drop from the tree. Then armed with heavy sticks we would hurl them up into the chestnut clusters. When they were ready they would shower down on us and we would scavenge the ground to see if any had popped and bounced from their encasements. I always went chestnutting with John and Joey. We never quarrelled about who was entitled to do what. Joey always threw the stick because he was good at it, he made it curl into the leaves, boomerang fashion. We would all search the ground if he had a direct hit. The nuts were pooled and we had a scrupulous count of them and a diligent share-out at the end of the day. Our parents were always pleased to receive them. They were a locally produced luxury. Fruit and nuts were scarce.

I've read about other children 'scrumping'. All that amounts to is stealing fruit from other people's fruit trees. There was little of that in our village, we were trained not to pick a pea or even a blackcurrant from someone else's garden, let alone venture out and raid an apple or a pear tree. Orchards were rare and the only one close to us came within the sanctified grounds of the Church of England. It belonged to the local vicar and most of the fruit was given away. Therefore it was not stolen, no bouquets would have been handed out to children who attempted to raid or scrump the vicarage orchard. Birds nested there, thrushes and blackbirds thrived as that wooded enclave was left in peace. The odd house possessed its own apple or pear tree, to rob these trees was tantamount to taking your life in your own hands. We knew where the trees were but never dared to trespass anywhere near them.

The town centre of Cannock was approximately one mile from where we lived. It had all the appearance of a country market town. There was a clock, a war memorial and an imposing church whose surrounding land and greenery took up a large slice of the commercial shopping centre. The church had a grand appearance — so grand that we never went in it.

It was the 'Cathedral' of the area and I don't think that many miners worshipped there. Joey was not afraid of its stature.

We were walking along the main approach road to the town centre. A high wall shut out the grounds of the vicarage from view. The fruit trees were loaded and some of their heavily laden branches over-shadowed the pavement. We walked under the fruit, aware of it but trying to pretend it didn't exist. Joey put an end to this hypocrisy.

'The pears aren't ripe.' He bent and picked up a bruised apple from the gutter. He rubbed the part of it that had not been battered on his sleeve, and then bit into it.

'These are ripe; here taste a bit.' He passed the apple on to John and me. We savoured a piece, it was sour-tasting but palatable and it was an apple and it was free. Joey stopped walking and stood beneath the tree. He looked up and surveyed the branches.

Joey was only a year older than John and me but sometimes he looked as old as my dad. He looked old now as he stared up at the tree, we went back and joined him. We knew what he was considering and we were afraid even before he told us. He must have known that we would be frightened. He had his argument ready, like an expert barrister he had prepared his case.

'They're not inside the grounds, they're outside. They're hanging on our side of the wall. They don't belong to anybody. Yes, yes they do. They belong to everybody that is walking on this side of the wall. It's the same if somebody's rose climbs into your garden. You can pick them because they're in your garden.'

'Nobody has touched them,' I pointed to the apples. It was a busy road and the many passers-by did not seem to observe the rights of property that Joey had declared. John was all for moving away from the temptation but Joey's fervour was triggered to a higher pitch by my remark.

'That's because they are grown-ups; most of them are anyway. They haven't had time to think about it.' (He had.) He had already found a sizeable stick and was testing it for weight. Unfortunately it seemed perfect for the operation.

His arm curved back as he took sight of his target, he grunted as he let the stick fly from his hand. There was a force behind Joey's throwing, he could hurl a stone further than anyone, his arms weren't fat but thin. Two apples broke from their moorings and we made unsuccessful attempts to catch them before they hit the ground. If we caught them before they bounced on the pavement, there would be no tell-tale bruise on the skins. John gathered both apples and folded them inside of his jersey. The stick clattered down afterwards, showering leaves on us as it fell near Joey's feet. Joey was right about the grown-ups, passers-by just stepped off the kerbstone and walked around us. None of them made any comment or criticised us for what we were doing. The second throw brought two more apples and the third delivered an avalanche. John and me were busy snatching them up as they dropped and rolled towards the gutter.

'Sod it, oh sod it. It's stuck, I can see it.' Joey's boomerang had lodged itself firmly in the boughs of the tree.

'I think we have enough,' John patted his jersey. It bulged with fruit, leaves were still floating down on us.

'Yes, we don't need any more,' I said.

Joey ignored us; he searched about for another stick.

'Not as good as the last one, but it will do,' he held up a piece of broken bough. Once more he took aim, we, the anxious gleaners of the operation, waited.

'You could hurt yourselves doing that; the stick might fall on your heads, it could poke one of your eyes out. You don't know where it is going to fall. This is a busy road, it could cause a car or a bus to crash, then other people would be hurt. You wouldn't want that to happen, now would you?' Joey lowered his arm to his side. We were so intent on looking up into the tree that we had not noticed the smartly dressed lady approach us. Without saying any more she took the stick from Joey's limp hand and chucked it over the church-yard wall. Weaponless, Joey gawped at her, more surprised than angry.

'We weren't doing anything wrong, missus,' he grumbled at her and kicked the floor with his feet.

'I didn't say you were, did I? Why don't you come to my house. I live just over there.' She pointed to a huge house with a large front garden. The house stood in its own grounds and had double bay windows. We followed her without question; we didn't know why we had been invited. Except that none of us felt uncomfortable, she hadn't sounded angry but cautionary. She hadn't shouted at us but had spoken quietly. Joey offered to carry her shopping bag and she accepted his changed conciliatory manner. She didn't say that we couldn't bring our apples with us. I had seen houses as large as hers, but I had never been in one. None of us had, so that we were curious and excited as she opened the front door and let us into the hallway.

We passed two doors as we trailed behind her, and an apple fell from under John's jersey; as he bent over to pick it up, his make-shift woollen envelope unsealed itself and the contents spilled on to the floor. They rolled in all directions. We were embarrassed by this and began to gather up our hoard as quickly as we could, mumbling apologies through our distress. She surprised us by laughing, she put her hand on Joey's shoulder.

'Leave them for now, I'll give you a carrier bag before you go. You can put them safely in that. Come, come,' she gestured with her hand, rings sparkled on her fingers. 'Here, sit in here, make yourselves comfortable in the lounge.' She opened one of the doors that led off the hallway.

'Would you like tea or lemonade?'

'Lemonade,' we chorused.

The room astonished us. It was twice as big as all the rooms put together in the house that I lived in. It was full of light because two large glass doors took up the whole of the end of it; through the doors there was a large room built of glass and beyond this was a long garden with two fruit trees in it. There was an enormous sofa and two large chairs covered with floral patterns. John sat in one of the chairs. It was so big that when he sat down in it he almost disappeared completely. For safety's sake, all three of us perched ourselves on the edge of the sofa. We didn't sit back because if we did our feet left the ground, and we couldn't see so well.

We talked about the contents of the place whilst she was out. There were three side-lights with Chinese shades and one light that was as tall as a man and this had an even bigger shade. There were pretty bowls of flowers, three carved wooden tables, sideboards with glass in them, full of china figures. There were statues on the mantelpiece and a clock which was held up by a shepherd and a shepherdess. The carpet covered every inch of the floor, it was a light fawn colour, but there were no marks on it. There were paintings hung on the walls; I couldn't tell what some of them were supposed to be — there was only one photograph. This was encased in a leather bound frame and stood on the sideboard. A man in an RAF uniform smiled from it. There was a lot to look at, but what attracted us most was the thing that hung from the ceiling above our heads.

It looked like a fountain that had been made out of glass. The sunlight brought out lots of different colours in it, and we gazed up at it as it shimmered over our heads. The crystals moved slightly, we were in awe of the object, silent, scarcely breathing. It even made slight chinking noises as the breeze from the open glass doors moved its glass.

'Oh, you like the chandelier?' the lady called from the glass room doorway. We nodded. 'I thought we'd have our lemonade here on the veranda.' She motioned for us to join her. Two new words, also new wonders, assailed my eyes and ears. Chandelier and veranda, I'd never heard these words before.

Chunks of ice floated in the lemonade. Where could she have got ice from at this time of year? We never had ice in any of our drinks at home. Her lemonade was better than any, perhaps it was because of the ice, or perhaps it was because of the large cut glasses with handles on both sides of them. We didn't know what to say to her after 'thank you' so we gulped at our drinks. She placed saucers on the white iron framed table that we sat around. I wanted to say something to her — acknowledge her kindness, but the glass surroundings, the iced lemonade, and her hair which was white but looked pale blue made me feel unusually shy. We left all the talking to her. From out of the floor inside the veranda a large green plant grew, it climbed up one side of the wall and spread its leaves all across the glass roof. She stood up, her clothes were plain. She wore brown flat shoes, a brown skirt, and a brown jumper. The only colourful thing about her was her hair. I wondered whether the hair was real or not, but then there was a lot about her house that might have seemed unreal if you hadn't seen it. She touched the thick twisted trunk of the plant.

'This is my vine,' she said, she patted it as though she were the proud owner of a champion horse or dog. 'And look, just look; look what it has produced. It's the first time; this year is the first time.'

'What are they missus? They're not plums are they?' Joey had seen plums growing and they didn't look at all like the cluster of dark red fruit which hung in a bunch from the roof of the veranda.

'My dears!' the woman exclaimed. She sounded shocked. 'Children — er — haven't you ever seen grapes before? That's what they're called, grapes.'

'I never seen one,' John murmured. Neither had I, but I wasn't going to admit it. The woman seemed to make a sudden decision. She got off her chair and placed it beneath the bunch of grapes. Joey marched gallantly forward and held the chair steady as she climbed on to it. She sawed at the vine with a bread-knife and cut away the whole lot of grapes. She washed them in cold water, then placed them in the middle of the table and rejoined us. She snipped at the grapes with some scissors. She didn't talk but made four small bunches out of the one big one.

'There, there, there and there, a few for each of us.' She placed the portions on the place before us.

'What about your husband, missus?' Joey asked.

'He'll have to wait until next year, won't he? Next year he can share them with my son when he comes home on leave. My son flies aeroplanes, he is a pilot.' This information impressed us so much that we didn't dare touch the grapes before us. The lady showed us what to do.

'Put the whole grape into your mouth, but don't swallow the pips. Just spit them out and place them on the side of your plate.' She demonstrated.

It did not take us very long to eat what was before us. You didn't have to chew this fruit, it burst in your mouth as your teeth crushed on it. It tasted sweet, it tasted good. Soon there were four plates of grape debris, a few sprigs of green, and lots of pips.

'We must go home now,' Joey said.

'Of course, of course, I'll get you a carrier bag for the apples.'

We collected all of the apples from the hallway and put them in the paper bag. Joey asked her if she wanted a few but she shook her head. John said that she looked as if she were going to cry but I told him to 'shurrup'. I knew that grown-ups hated children seeing them cry. Anyway, she didn't cry, she suddenly smiled brightly and said what nice boys we were. She saw us down to her front gate and waved to us as we left her.

My mother accepted the apples. She said they were cooking apples but that she would make something with them. 'No, the lady never asked us our names and she never told us hers.' I had given my mother a detailed account of the afternoon's wonderment. She was very interested when I described the inside of the house. Two or three times I had to describe the ... what was it called? The chandelier. 'A chandelier, what about that eh, a chandelier,' she muttered as I talked on.

8

Darts

The Utic's Nest is a funny name for a pub. If a Utic had a nest then it must have been a bird. I'd never heard of a bird called a Utic and nobody else had, but that was the name of the public house just down the road from where we lived. If you asked anyone what a Utic was, they just shrugged their shoulders or shook their heads as though you were asking a daft or silly question. A pub was a pub and its name obviously was of little account or interest to its customers. I would never have gone there in the first place if my mother's working shifts had not been changed. She worked 'nights' in a factory in Darlaston. For some reason, she was required to work on a Saturday night. This gave her Wednesday and Thursday night free. It changed the lean social arrangements that my parents were limited to — the Saturday night at the Working Men's Club was now in abeyance.

It was substituted by a Thursday night visit to 'The Utic's Nest'. I suppose that in accordance with licensing laws children should have been barred entrance. They never were; the licensee did not seem at all uncomfortable when the local bobby came in for a pint. There were other children there besides me, either the policeman didn't mind or he chose not to see us. In any event, we were always limited to one bottle of Vimto and a bag of crisps. If you took little sips the bottle lasted all night. I never shared my crisps, nor did I join the other children who sat and talked quietly around a large table set apart in the end of the pub, well away from the bar. The pub only possessed one very long, oblong-shaped room and everything that went on happened in it. I usually sat to the right of my father, he on a chair, me on a stool. My mother always faced us, her back resting on the wall. The three or four couples that joined them at their table never varied much. Sometimes one of my aunties or uncles would join us, but they never stayed long. I would listen to the grown-ups talk, the men talked to men and the women talked to women.

Neither paid much heed to me, I didn't expect them to. Occasionally one of the men would say, 'Alright then Tom lad?' and nod his head. The women might say, 'You've got a Wakefield look but your mam's eyes.' There really wasn't much that I could say to these acknowledgments so I kept quiet. I was never bored. Other things happened at The Utic's Nest.

Each night a man would play the piano for a short time and at the end of his repertoire there would be a call for a song. It was always the same lady. And she always sang the same song. She was fat, older than my parents, and her name was Mrs Welch. She was a widow. She wore a black dress with sequins decorating its bosom. The song was called 'Love's Last Word is Spoken, Cherie'. She sang it beautifully and at the end she never failed to wipe her eyes as she had moved herself to tears by the quality of her own performance. Some of the women in the pub cried a little too — but not my mother. She did clap though and would say 'lovely voice, Elsie has a lovely voice.'

A darts match was also played. The Utic's Nest was part of a kind of league. If other teams lost at The Utic's Nest there was always an undercurrent of dissent or grumbling. Not that the game had been played unfairly but on account of the four members who made up the darts team. All of them wore trousers, all of them wore shirts. But two of the players had trousers which buttoned down the side, no fly-hole in the front. These two also had breasts, but their hair was short. They were known as Billy and Mac. They were well liked at The Utic. They would always greet my parents and often buy me an extra bag of crisps or supply me with another bottle of Vimto. Sometimes, they would ruffle my hair but they never said much. In fact, I hardly ever saw them a yard apart from one another. They puzzled me.

If I wanted to know something, mostly I would ask my father. He knew everything about everybody in the pub. I don't know what prompted me to interrogate my mother. I half expected a curt reply. I was surprised.

'Mam, those two, Billy and Mac, are they men or women?' She paused and sipped at her milk stout, licked the froth from the top of her lip and looked at me directly.

'They're good people,' she said.

'Are they men or women?' Other women around the table had heard me repeat the question. I think they were as interested in her response as I was.

'They're willdews,' she said.

'Willdews, willdews, what's a willdew?' She threw back her head and chortled, this was rare for her and I thought that she had dismissed my question with her mirth.

'Well, it's like this. They are ladies, they'll never be anything else. But they won't marry because they live together in a bungalow. And when they are at home it must be "will yer do this or will yer do that". Got it? So, they are willdews.' At this the other women laughed. I still did not understand but accepted the explanation. However, she did not let it end there. She addressed the other women.

'That's why the other teams get upset, well some of them do if they lose. Behave like bloody little kids, grown men, yes they do. I don't know why. Their lives are their own, as I say, they're good women.'

'Oh, I know that Esther, we'd never get ambulance drivers like those two ever again. They were ever so good when they took my mother to Stafford hospital. Do you know, they even took her in some flowers on the Sunday. Off duty they were, it was their day off. My mother said they were golden, yes, she said that to me about them before she died. And Esther, I think you're right, people often sling a bit of squitch in their direction — but they've no grounds for it. No, they wouldn't do anybody any harm. They are good, they mind their own business and lead their own lives. They'd help anybody yer know.' The other women nodded respectfully.

It was later that I noticed that when an opposing team lost, one or two of the losing men would say something nasty to Billy or Mac. Billy and Mac ignored the insults but the men did not get away free. One of the married women sitting drinking would hurl abuse at them, others would join in and Billy and Mac basked in their defence. After a time, no man dared say bad things to them. But my dad told me that Billy and Mac were only allowed to play in home games, not away games, not in other pubs. Darts was a man's game. It seemed that Billy and Mac could only fit in at The Utic's Nest. They were always there — every Thursday.

9

The GIs

We never travelled much, there wasn't anywhere to travel to. To an outsider's eye, our world might have seemed confined, parochial, but we had space, a lot of space. Even the known was oddly unfamiliar, it might have been the geography or the landscape. An uneasy landscape for a child. The mining area incorporated stark contrasts of steady inclines and huge patches of woodland. There were tiny thumbs of local industry but not much, for the most part it was cramped rows of houses, the lanes, the woodlands, strange water pools, canals, moors and the coal mines. So you see, with just a fragment of imagination we could be anywhere we chose to be, if we thought about it hard enough.

There were places where we never went. One pool in particular, it was known as the 'Cat and Dog'. Unlike other pools (many of them beautiful testaments to an abandoned 'jack pit'), this pool, the 'Cat and Dog', was not renowned for its fishing. It wasn't stagnant, but none of us swam there or played near it. My father said it had got its reputation before his time. The pool was or had been a burial ground for unwanted puppies and kittens. These creatures were placed in a sack weighted with stones, the top of the sack strung tight, and then . . . . I never saw anybody do that, but I suppose they did. A doctor was expensive, let alone a vet. I never went near the pool, nor did my friends. In this way it achieved all the reverence of a cemetery, except that the reverence was based on fear. But then, people don't go to cemeteries at night time, do they? Not even grown-ups.

And fear kept us from Gaskin's Wood. Murder had been done there. It had happened before I was born, but every child knew the story. My dad told me about it.

'Ah, his name was Gaskin. Not a name you can get out of your head, is it? He was a miner, a local chap. He killed his own wife. Hold on, he didn't stop at that. Oh, no, oh, no, he cut her up into pieces. An arm off, a leg off, her head off. Then he took each piece. Each piece separate mind you, and buried the bits in different places in the wood. Well, they found most of her bit by bit. They caught him, and he was hanged.'

Gaskin's Wood was small, an untrained pine wood, no grown-ups went there either, people weren't curious about that kind of thing. The wood bore his name and even lovers in their first passions were never tempted to take cover under its mystery and darkness.

Apart from these bleak overtones, visitors met a changing landscape, one that combined countryside with a harsh mining industry. We had lots of visitors. Strangers, some people called them. Immigrants I suppose. Yes, then at that time Cannock Chase was cosmopolitan. There were Bevin Boys from all over Britain; and some men who had to work down the mines because they didn't like the idea of killing anybody, even if it was a German. They spoke English but spoke it different from us. Then there were very, very tall men, these were Polish refugees, many of these married and stayed. There were men from the RAF camp; prisoners of war from Italy. Last of all came the GIs. Americans, real Americans that spoke like the people we saw at the pictures.

Not one of them that I saw looked like Flash Gordon, but he was special and you couldn't have expected him to have come to us with all the dangerous things that he had to do each week.

Now, all the American soldiers that I had seen on the pictures were white. Any black people I had seen had either been servants, tap-dancers, or they played banjos. None of the black soldiers did any of these things. We stopped singing one of our skipping rhymes.

In the kitchen, in the house,
A black man will get you if you don't watch out
OUT spells out!

The first black man that I saw was dressed in a smart uniform. He was a sergeant. He didn't carry a spear. I said to him what all of us children said to the GIs, 'Got any gum chum?' We begged like this a lot. We were rarely refused and the black sergeant gave me a whole packet. Not just a strip of chewing gum, a whole packet he gave me.

The GIs didn't stay too long, a few months and then they had gone. I was sorry, most of the children were sorry. Some of the older girls were too, but instead of putting sand and water on their legs some of them were left with silk stockings. Funny that I should think about the GIs after they had left. It all happened on a Sunday.

A bottle of lemonade or orangeade was a big treat that went with our Sunday dinner. I was sent up to the off-licence to collect a full bottle and return an empty one. At mid-day the shop was always crowded. I didn't mind this. I loved to hear grown-ups talking. The people serving behind the counter never seemed to hurry, they took their time and chatted with each customer. Sunday was not a day for being hasty, and the people in the shop waited. Some sat on small empty wooden barrels, others perched their behinds on up-turned empty crates. People talked, it was a cheerful noisy place. I never pushed forward to get served before my time. Sometimes I lingered on and sat there, letting the odd one or two people push in front of me. My eyes watched the jugs being filled with beer. The pump handles were of shiny brass, and it was fun to watch Mr Hapley pull them and fill the jug at the same time that he was talking. The beer never overflowed − I looked out for it to spill over the top of the jug but it never did. I looked and I listened. Mr Hapley was a master of the pumps.

When Elaine Braithwaite came in, people began to speak more quietly. And then, they stopped talking altogether. Not even a whisper. She stood at the back of the crowd. I sat on the crate and looked at her. That's what everyone in the shop was doing, looking at her. I knew that she had left school because she had worked on the milk round. She must have been quite old, at least seventeen. She had blonde hair but her face which was usually of a rosy colour on account of her job was white and pale. Her eyes were fixed, like the blind lady's were in Hancock Street. She rested back on her heels. Her belly was ever so big. She held her bag over it, not as if she were trying to hide anything. Her belly was so big it looked as though it would burst.

My friend Jimmy Harvey had told me that you could only have babies if you were married. And he said that you dropped out of your mam's fanny when it got big enough. At first I didn't like this story, but I knew it was true because it had happened to Queenie who lived next door to us. He said that sometimes, if the belly got big enough, you could have two babies at a time. I accepted the half-mystery. I knew that I hadn't come from under a gooseberry bush. That's what my parents had told me the first time I asked. And I knew that I hadn't been delivered in Nurse Wainwright's black bag. That was the second story they had told me. No, it was a grown-up secret, Jimmy Harvey had found out the truth. Babies did come from women's bellies.

Elaine Braithwaite was having one. I could see that she

was. What puzzled me was . . . well, Elaine wasn't married. She stood there, right near me. I wanted to put my ear to her belly. Instead I touched her arm — lightly, and moved over on the crate so that she could sit next to me. For the first time, she moved her head, looked down at me and smiled in a queer sort of way and shook her head; then stared at nothing again. That shop had gone so quiet and still. All that you could hear was the swishing noise of the beer pumps.

'A pint of mild is it Elaine?' Mr Hapley called out to her. She was last in and first served. Nobody complained. They made way for her as she waddled forward.

'And a bag of crisps please,' she said, then she walked out of the shop as though she had been the only person in it. The door closed behind her, then the talking started.

'Yes, her dad gave her a terrible hiding, strapped her, and her mother has threatened to throw her out.' There were whispers amongst some of the women.

'No!'

'So they say, oh yes. And look at her, not a trace of shame, bold as brass and her mouth clamped up like a bloody vice.'

'A black baby, a black baby, what in hell is she going to do with it. Oh, her poor mother. I know what I'd do with her if she were my daughter. I bloody do. What's she going to do with it . . . .'

'God knows, I've heard say he wants to marry her.'

'Marry her! Have a black man touching . . . oh Ina. That dirty little cat, I don't know how she could, the thought of it, oh . . . .'

'She were seen with him. She were warned. Now look what it's come to.'

'I mean, how could you let a black man er touch and . . . .'

'Shush, shush, sh, sh,' one of the older women indicated that two children were present, me and another boy.

Mr Hapley served us next. The other boy left before me. I could see that they were waiting for me to leave. I flipped and fumbled with the door latch, wanting to hear more. I needn't have bothered with the delaying tactics. They waited. I was denied.

'It smells in here,' it was all I could think to say. I liked Elaine. 'Now you get out Tommy, I'll tell your mother what you've said and you'll be larruped for being cheeky.' Ina pointed her finger at me.

I couldn't answer her, I left quickly and banged the door loudly as I shut it behind me. If I had been a black baby, I think I would have fought all those women in that shop. But babies can't fight can they? The ones I had seen all looked the same to me. I would have liked to have seen Elaine's baby, it would have been bound to have looked different.

That afternoon we sang at Sunday school. I loved the songs; we did actions to some of them. 'Now think of someone who might need help, sing up, sing loud and ask God while you sing to do what the song says. Think of somebody else, not of yourself.' Mr Jones conducted whilst we sang

> Throw out the life-line, throw out the life-line,
> Someone is sinking today.
> Throw out the life-line, throw out the life-line,
> Someone is sinking toda a a a y.

My line went in Elaine's direction. It must have done. She did marry the black man. She left Cannock. They said she went to live with him in America, but nobody knew for sure because she never wrote to anyone. Her mam or dad wouldn't mention her name.

Later, my dad told me that lots of black men were fighting in the war — on our side, and he said that a black man was the fastest runner in the world, faster than any Englishman or German. So I asked him, straight out.

'Is it dirty to have a black baby?'

'Yer what our Tom?'

'Dad, is it dirty to have a black baby?' I was persistent. He

65

looked puzzled, shook his head, scratched his ear. He wasn't going to tell a grown-up lie.

'There's nothing dirty about havin' any kind of baby. Who've you been talking to?'

'Nobody dad,' I replied truthfully. I wished I could have seen Elaine Braithwaite again. If I had, I would have told what my dad told me. I suppose she knew anyway; as I say she looked pale, but not frightened. Oh no, she didn't look frightened.

10

Frolic

Within a mile of my village, there were no less than seven cinemas. In the major town of Cannock, there was the Danilo, the Forum, and the Picture House. At Hednesford there was the Tivoli and the Empire. At the village of Heath Hayes there was the Picture House and a few hundred yards from where I lived was the Blackford's Central Cinema. The Central Cinema was the smallest of them all, it had no balcony and it could not have seated many more people than two hundred at capacity. That's if you chose to put one person on one seat.

At one time, I had been told that it had been a garage. It never looked like one to me, and I found this difficult to believe. None of the cinemas were expensive and they often changed their programme twice a week. I was allowed to go one night out of every week. Usually this was a Wednesday. The choice was always a difficult one as there was so much to choose from. Further agony was supplied if there were two films that you were desperate for, I often felt cheated by the programme change. I never went to the Central Cinema during my evening visits; the more recent and exciting films were always showing elsewhere.

Saturday afternoon was a lucky-dip, because that was the afternoon that the Central Cinema had their matinée. Only children attended. Lengthy queues began to line up long before the programme started. For threepence you gained admittance, you never knew what film you were going to see. So there was always a surprise in store, one way or another. There was one main feature film shown and a serial. Cowboy films were the most popular — everybody liked Johnny Mack Brown except me, I only liked cowboy films if there were Indians in them. Shocks were not infrequent. Films that I thought I might like sometimes frightened me. We all cheered when *Snow White and the Seven Dwarfs* announced itself on the screen. But some of us were frightened by it and I had bad dreams about it for weeks.

Compensation came in other ways. Musicals were booed before they began, but sometimes we were enraptured. How we all cried and cheered through *Meet Me in St Louis* and it was nearly all about girls and there was singing and kissing, but we liked it. Every time Margaret O'Brien appeared we clapped and there was no way that we could recognise Judy Garland from her *Wizard of Oz* days. A new, smaller, younger child was the star in our firmament. We liked Margaret O'Brien because she was naughty and because she had accidents and then we could feel sorry for her.

After the 'big' film was over we were treated to the serial. Nobody could compete with Flash Gordon for popularity. He was greeted with huge accolades every time he stepped out of a space ship and the wicked emperor 'Ming' was always hissed at. If the 'big' film was dull, the cinema got very noisy, so noisy that it was impossible to hear the sound track. We were troublesome for two reasons, if the film was boring we lost interest and when we lost interest we became acutely aware of our discomfort. You see, no matter how many children turned up for the Saturday matinée, none were ever turned away. So that we were crushed together sometimes two or three children on one seat. It got very hot in that cinema, and water trickled down the walls. We would write our names on the wetness when the show was over.

There were two middle-aged usherettes and they had marvellous discipline, considering that they always managed to keep us in our seats.

'Quiet, quiet, qu-i-e-t, or out you go, and you, and you,' they would point and bawl when things got a bit out of hand. One of the usherettes was called 'Squirter'. It wasn't her real name, but that's what we called her. Our name was not an unfair one because she did squirt, sometimes two or three times during every show. You could hear it before the smell — a sickly, scented smell settling in a cloud about your head. 'Squirter' would take ten or more paces down one side aisle (there was no middle one) and then pump a haze of this stuff over our heads. I watched her at her squirting — she seemed to enjoy it. The instrument looked like a large bicycle pump with a can attached to the underside of its sprayer. The end of the pump was like the end of a watering can. She pulled the pump handle back and then let it rip. For a few moments the screen appeared foggy as something akin to fine rain fell about us. Then the smell came. I don't think that the audience whiffed as bad as the odour that settled. She was a diligent lady and did both aisles, so that wherever you sat, throughout the performance you were subjected to this sweet-stinking fog. I never got used to it. Dead hyacinths, that was what the smell was like.

'You'll have to start early, eight o'clock in the morning. Finish it round about half-past four or five o'clock. I'll give you three shillings and any broken cakes that are left over.' Saturday jobs were difficult to come by, there was a list of boys waiting for someone to give up a paper round. The milkman already had a helper. It was Mr Skeghorn who delivered the bread who was making me the offer. I wanted the job, the money would be more than useful. But I stood apprehensively on the foot of the pavement as he stared down at me from his seat on the bread cart. He was perched quite high up, it was a big cart, with big wheels and the horse that pulled it was enormous. Mr Skeghorn held the reins and waited for my answer. I was afraid of the horse. Its size frightened me. Mr Skeghorn saw me glance at the huge hooves of the animal.

'Don't tell me you're scared of Frolic. There's not a bad thought in this old girl's head.' As if to prove his point, he jumped down from his driving seat and passed under the horse's belly, this way, then that way. The horse did not move. Mr Skeghorn took my hand and led me under the belly past the great hooves and out the other side.

'Now do it on your own,' he said.

Feeling ill with fright, I passed under the creature's belly and got myself on to the pavement on the other side.

'Want the job then?'

'Yes, please.' I was still unsure

'Hop on then,' he commanded.

I could just about get my foot on the iron stand, by hopping on the other one I was able to grab the side handle of the cart and haul myself on to the cart's chassis. I sat next to him. I looked down, we were a long way from the ground, it was better to look forward. I had a marvellous view of Frolic's massive behind. It was so big, I'd never seen that part of a horse before, not at such close quarters. Mr Skeghorn made a clicking noise with his mouth, and called out 'Come on then old girl, come on then old girl.' Frolic waved her head a little, pricked her ears and moved forward pulling me, Mr Skeghorn, and a load of bread and cakes behind her.

It felt strange travelling along so high up, I got used to it more quickly than I imagined and had reached the state of actually enjoying the experience when it was time to climb down. The houses were all bunched close together, there was no point in climbing up again as this would have delayed delivery of the bread. Frolic understood English, although she couldn't speak it. If we had progressed ahead of her without bread baskets Mr Skeghorn would shout 'Here girl, here girl.' She would plod forward and stop just where he wanted her to, he didn't have to touch the reins or anything like that. While we were delivering bread, he didn't talk to me at all — only the horse. He had worked out his own sign language with regard to what type of bread I should take to each house. He said that this language was quicker than talking. He said he didn't have to think and I was expected to know what the signs meant after only one run through. I have never forgotten them.

If he tapped the top of his head it meant one large loaf; two taps of the head meant two large white loaves. The taps indicated the numbers required. A flick on his nose meant a small white loaf. A smack on his chest or breast meant a milk loaf and he would smack his behind and smile if a brown loaf was required. The combinations could be quite involved and I had to pay great attention to his signals before I loaded my basket. One tap of the head, two taps of the breast and a smack on the bum meant one large white loaf, two milk loaves, and one brown loaf. I was always required to ask of each customer 'Any cakes, missus?' This was important as Mr Skeghorn got a small bonus if he managed to sell over a certain amount of cakes. I think he almost always got that bonus, we somehow managed to sell most of the confectionary between us. He was a very fair man, because if there were any cakes left over, he would break a few in order that he could honour our contract. He would always place these fragments in a bag for me.

Our round covered three villages and it was the space between each village which allowed us the luxury of riding on the cart. None of the villages were more than a mile apart, so that our transit was mainly on foot. This made the riding section of the job even more precious than ever. I think Mr Skeghorn enjoyed these bits of the job as much as I did.

It was only during these periods that he would open his mouth to speak. Mr Skeghorn loved Frolic; at times the mare appalled me. The horse would fart loudly, and I would hate this as it was directed right into our faces, even worse, sometimes it would steady itself, slow its pace, its arse would open up before our eyes and great dollops of shit would steam forth out of it. I never came to terms with this, but Skeghorn greeted this with pleasure. 'That's it girl, let it to, they'll have big brussel sprouts in this street this year.' Then he would shout 'Gardens! Gardens!' Immediately a man or a woman would run out from somewhere with a shovel and bucket and retrieve what Frolic had left behind.

'There's your proof,' he said.

'What of? Proof what of?' I asked him.

'That horses are the best of creatures, better than dogs, cats, you or me.' I could not understand his reasoning and said so. He looked at me with a painful sorrowing glance as if I ought to have understood and not questioned his assumption.

'Everything about a horse is useful. Dog shit, cat shit, my shit or your shit would kill anything if they got near it; put it on a garden and the plants would die. Have you ever seen people manuring their gardens by squatting amongst the potatoes and shitting on it themselves?'

'No,' I said.

'Well, there you are then, there's nothing bad about a horse, even its shit is a good thing. That's more than can be said about you or me.' Mr Skeghorn did love his horse.

'You've never seen a pit pony, have yer?' I shook my head.

'No, you wouldn't see one unless you'd been down the pit. I've seen them — poor buggers, never see the light of day, go blind they do, and some of 'um are just lathered to death before they're brought up and then put down.'

'Put down?'

'Yes, bloody shot, the poor buggers are good for sod all once they've done a stint down there. They kill 'um. That's why I left the pits. Some say it was because I didn't like hard work. Not true, not true, I've always liked horses, any kind of horses, and it made me feel bad, right bad the way the ponies were treated. I've been on this round nearly three years now. Come on Frolic old girl, come on, we aye got all day yer know. We've all got homes to go to.' He would make his clicking noise, but never use the reins or the bit, a whip or the thought of striking a horse would probably have made him ill again. He had seen ponies blind and beaten and one of his major missions in life seemed to be Frolic's happiness and contentment in her job. No one will believe this but I felt that after a few months of working with him Mr Skeghorn closely resembled his best friend, the Shire mare called Frolic. He never talked about his wife or two daughters — he did have a family, my mother had told me about them. He either talked to me about the work, or he talked to the horse directly. His habits were much the same as the mare's.

The mare would sometimes push the bit forward from her mouth, probably in order to get the iron clamp more comfortably placed. Skeghorn, in his occasional pensive moments would push out the top dentures of his false teeth, they never fell out of his jaw but he gave his gums a rest in much the same way as the horse did. He would snort like the horse too, particularly when we only had a few more calls to make before finishing. It was his way of sighing — horse-like. Also, when he felt the need he would lift his left or right buttock and fart explosively. He never said sorry to me or anything like that but if one were extra loud, he would chortle to himself, then shout to the mare — 'Catch that one Frolic, beat that one old girl.' The first time he did it I stared at him in a hostile way, but he took no notice of me. And I just accepted it all after a matter of weeks.

I forgot about the picture matinée, I could choose to see two films a week now. I was in a position to discern now that my economic situation had dramatically improved.

Strange, I didn't always go twice a week, in the summer

months I even missed a week or even a fortnight of visits to the cinema. I began to save money, but there was no purpose in mind for its spending. I worked with Skeghorn for nearly two years and I don't think he asked me a single question about myself. He once asked me to take the harness and halter from the horse, but the mare shivered when I patted her neck, and twitched as I began to unbuckle the heavy girth belts. Skeghorn patted my shoulder, he must have sensed my fears and took pity on me. 'Leave it to me, Tom,' he said gently. Of course, he might have been feeling more sorry for his mare than me. She didn't like a stranger handling her, that was clear.

'Well, this will be yer last day.' That was how he announced my dismissal one Saturday morning. I wondered if I had done anything wrong, or he had found another lad to help him. We had not formed a relationship, but I felt a little hurt, well more than a little, as I was efficient at my job. He waited before we came to a halt before he gave me an explanation. Then I could see he was upset. He pushed his dentures forward, so far I thought that they would fall to the ground.

He took off his thick glasses and wiped the lenses over and over again with his handkerchief.

'The baker is going over to vans. Vans that you drive. They've offered us driving lessons. They're not catching me with a fucking van, I'm not driving a van. No, I'm not.' He put his glasses on and made a snorting noise. I couldn't look at him, I climbed down from the cart and called out from the side aperture, he remained where he was, it was easier to question him unseated.

'What are you going to do, Mr Skeghorn? Will you get another job? What about Frolic?' It was only the last question which seemed to give him any concern.

'Well, they say they're giving — yes — giving all these Shire horses to farmers; but farmers don't use big horses like this nowadays. In any case, this old girl is trained for what she's at now, she's not going to take easy to a ploughed field, is she? No, I reckon they'll put her down.'

'Can't you stop them Mr Skeghorn, that's not right.' I cried out.

'No lad, it's not right, it's not, but I'm a nobody. I can't stop them doing it, I can't. It's making me feel bad and sick.' He climbed from the platform and joined me. He filled two large bags full of cakes (not breaking one of them) and gave them to me. He handed me five shillings.

'We've only just started the round, Mr Skeghorn,' I wanted to say something to comfort him, but we had never talked in that way. Feelings had never come into things of a Saturday.

'Well, I want to do the round on my own today — just me and Frolic. Now give the cakes to your mama and don't blab to anyone that I gave you them. Go on, off you go now lad, you'll be in time for the threepenny rush this afternoon!'

I took the cakes, took the extra money and left him without saying goodbye. I gave my mother the cakes and told her what had happened.

'Are you going to the matinée this afternoon?' she asked.
'No.'

'I didn't think you would,' she said.

II

White Hot

Other people had knocked on the door and asked her if she were coming out. 'In a minute, in a minute, I'll be out in a minute,' she had replied pleasantly. I watched her. She was making no attempt to move from her position near the fire. She was too near and her legs had become mottled by the heat. She seemed unaware of this. All the rest of the street were out, all the children, all the mothers. I didn't want to go to the VE party unless my mother was there singing and wearing a paper hat like all the other mums. I required her presence at the festivities; if she were not there, then I couldn't anticipate the enjoyment. We had almost won the war. It was nearly over. We were expected to sing and dance. A party, a street party was in progress and my mother was sitting crouched over the fire.

I didn't ask her to come out but she knew well enough why I chose to sit and sulk and read comics in the corner. She picked up the poker and thrust it deep into the fire. This was a habit of hers. I would like to think that it was based on economics because when the end of the poker was white-hot with heat she would hold it close to her face and light a cigarette with it. Matches were saved in this way. However, sometimes she just withdrew the poker and let it cool without lighting a cigarette. From time to time, I would peer over the edge of my comic, waiting for some movement from her. The poker was still in its place, one end wedged deeply in the embers of the coal, the handle sticking out somewhere near her shins.

All the other women in our row of houses liked my mother. She never gossiped. Queenie and Amelia would have gladly died for her. I couldn't understand their loyalty. I was not able to recognise either illness or integrity. Both Queenie and Amelia were out with the other women, singing and dancing and being happy. The two women had popped in and not cajoled my mother.

'If you feel like it then Esther,' was all that they had said in the way of persuasion.

My mother looked up from the fire. I pretended that I was unaware of the fact that she was looking in my direction. I held the comic up and covered my face from her gaze. I could never fool her, not in the same way as I could my dad on occasions.

'I'm not stopping you from going. The party has started,' she used her flat voice. I punished her by not answering and merely turned over another page of the comic.

'What are you sulking about?' she asked.

'Same as you, I'm being the same as you.' I snapped at her, to my surprise she did not reply. She picked up a newspaper that lay at her feet, she only seemed interested in looking at one page. She would look at this page and then place it back on the floor again, only to glance at it again a few minutes later. That's all she was doing, looking at that page, then staring into the fire.

If she were in this preoccupied state, I would often try to dispose of it by drawing her attention to something I had read in a book, or even tell her the content of the play I had listened to on radio's *Saturday Night Theatre*, she liked hearing me tell these modern fables. Sometimes I would ginger up the plot a bit by adding some on. In her present mood I felt no sympathy for her, merely irritation. When I felt like this, I usually resorted to provocation. Anger I found more palatable than the silence. She would shout when provoked and call me a little 'snipe', which, I suppose, is what I was. She reached for her knitting.

'You're not going to knit, are you? We've all got too many pullovers. You use the wrong colours anyway, the Fair Isle pullover you did last time is bumpy where the patterns are; it doesn't fit in the right places.'

'Don't wear it then.'

'I won't. I won't wear it. "Did yer mam knit that Tommy?"' I mimicked a neighbour. 'Yes, my clever, non-talking mam did it. All on her own — four needles, ever so difficult.'

I tried to sting some action into her, but my taunting had a reverse effect. She put the knitting back in its place and spoke into the air. She didn't sound angry. 'She's a nice woman, Mrs Millington.' My acting had been good, my mother had detected whom I was impersonating. Her bland response made me furious. I screwed my comic into a ball and hurled it on to the fire. She was forced to back away a little as the flames rose.

'I won't order it next week now. I won't order them for you ever again. You can just read books. Books without pictures, it's no loss seeing how clever you are.' She was angry now, but her voice she kept low.

'I'll show you some bloody pictures. Just sit where you are; don't you dare move or you'll get a crack on the head.' She meant it. I sat still, quiet, defiant. 'There, stuff your eyes into that lot and don't forget what you've seen. And if you have bad dreams so much the better — because that's the only way you'll ever remember what this has all been about. People are going to forget; people forget everything with time.' She thrust the newspaper on to my lap.

On a closer scrutiny, it wasn't a daily paper at all; it was bits of pages from three or four papers, the *Herald*, the *Express*, the *News Chronicle*, the *Mail*, they were all represented. Stranger still, some of them were dated 1944. Today was 8 May 1945. It was VE Day. Outside in the street, tables had been dragged out to spell out the letters in a weird geometry, the celebrations had commenced, people were singing and whooping with delight. We could hear them. And here I was with my mother expecting me to look at some papers that were dated 1944. I tried to resist looking at them.

But the first two pictures on one of the papers drew my attention — horror always arouses curiosity. One of the photographs showed a man curled like a coloured snake and ensnared between sections of barbed wire. His head hung down, so that his feet pointed into the air. The barbs on the wire held him in this splayed, petrified position. He wore striped clothing and there was a star printed on his arm.

'Has he been shot mam?' I was already chastened.

'No, you can read what it says; the wire is electrified. He's dead. Electrocuted.'

'What, what did he want to jump on the barbed wire for?' I couldn't see the sense in his action. She answered me as if I were an adult. I deserved it, I had goaded her into it.

'If you had been inside a Nazi Concentration Camp, you might have felt happier ending up on the barbed wire than being part of what was going on inside. I would have done.'

'You wouldn't have thrown yourself on the wire!'

'Yes, I think I could — but you never know. There are other pictures,' she waved her hand.

The next one was one I could identify with. In all pictures or films of the war, it was usually our men or women fighting and winning or losing and dying bravely. These pictures were different. Children had never been shot in any films that I had seen. But there on the same page as the man impaled on the barbed wire was a photograph of a boy. He was holding up his hands, he was wearing clothes like mine, he had a cap like me and he didn't look at all different from me, his face even resembled mine. He looked very frightened.

'They're going to shoot him. He's dead now,' she said.

'Germans?' I asked.

'Nazis, Nazis,' she spat out the words. 'Nazis don't have to be Germans, they can be anybody, their feelings are rotten.'

The last photograph was enough, I looked at it and closed the paper. At first, I thought it must have been the inside of an old slave ship — there were people lying on bunk beds, some half naked, all pathetically thin and emaciated, you couldn't tell whether or not they were dead or alive. 'Are they men or women?' even their sexuality seemed to have disappeared and I had not thought this possible, but I couldn't distinguish the differences in gender although I knew what points to look for. These people were shrunken, the parts that might have given some clue were indistinguishable and all their heads were shaved.

'Both. They're men and women, or they were at some time. They were just like us; that's what the Nazis have done to them. It's not only soldiers who have gone under in this bloody war yer know.' She buried her head in her hands. I wanted to put my arms around her. Comfort her, kiss her neck or lick her ear. But she had never shown me physical affection and would not have appreciated me expressing any towards her. She didn't like to be touched by me. Yet I wanted to touch her. I couldn't reach her suffering but I had glimpsed some of the depths of it — thanks to the horrible photographs. It dawned then, it entered my head then, that my mother was clever, she thought about things but had no one to talk to about them. Her injuries were buried within her. I had discovered a nest with eggs in.

'Never mind mam, we've beaten the Nazis now. Germany is conquered, our armies have won.' I spoke in a conciliatory, patriotic manner. I had forgotten the party, the noise outside was still going on but my concern was for her. She took little solace from my general and popular observation.

'You don't think that Nazis will ever go away, just like that,' she snapped her fingers. 'They're still there; there's some in all countries. There are Nazis in this country, they'll be back. People forget, I've told you once, people forget. They'll start their bloody marching all over again. I know it; you'll see, mark my words. People forget, they shouldn't, but they do.'

I passed the papers back to her and sat next to her, cross-legged on the rug. I got as close to her as possible without touching her. We both looked into the fire. There was a tap on the window pane. Amelia's face looked in on us, she smiled at us, beckoned us to come out. My mother waved, smiled and nodded.

'I'll stop in with you if you like mam. Or if you want — I'll go out on my own.' These words brought tears to her face, she did not wish me to see her cry and quickly brushed the drops away with the back of her hand. She leapt up as though I'd jabbed a pin in her bum.

'Come on, it's party time. I'll take me pinafore off and go out in me pyjamas. That'll give them a laugh. I'll wear your dad's cap and you can wear my best one; the one with feathers in it. Put it on back-to-front and you'll look like Robin Hood.' She had already begun to change and had fetched in the hat before I could wholeheartedly respond to the change in mood. Her histrionics were powerful when turned on. I had the hat, it was precious.

'They might get broken, the feathers might . . . '

'Oh, bugger the feathers; out we go for a "Knees up Mother Brown",' she cried.

She jammed the hat on my head and turned me around and pushed me so that I could see myself in the sideboard mirror. We both looked funny and I began to laugh. She went to leave. I called her back.

'The poker, it's still in the fire. You've left it sticking in the fire.'

For a few seconds she lost her false verve and éclat, she bent down to the grate and removed the iron from the fire and placed it carefully in the hearth. Then we both left to join the festivities.

The poker remained in the hearth still white-hot. In the meantime we danced, and sang, and ate, and laughed. When we returned the poker had cooled and it was necessary for her to heat it up in order to light a cigarette.

12

Change of Scene

'Ah've booked, ah've booked us up for a week's holiday. Not a day trip, no, I've booked us up for a week at Blackpool. All of us, the deposit is paid and the rest will be in the landlady's hand when we arrive. I've got a nice letter from her, seems a good woman. We have bed, breakfast, dinner and tea — it's all in the price.' My father waved the letter in the air. 'We have two rooms,' he added. 'One for you and me' (he nodded to my mother) 'and our Tom shares a room with three other kids who come from West Bromwich.'

'Who are they dad — the lads from West Bromwich?' I asked.

'I don't know our Tom. How should I know anybody from West Bromwich?'

'You can stay at home if you don't want to come,' my mother had caught the semblance of a frown on my brow.

'I do want to come,' I said quickly.

'That's that then, we're off on August Bank Holiday. We'll go by train from Stafford. Just four months away, and Bert Miles says we're in for a good summer this year,' he said sounding pleased with himself.

'How does he know what the summer is going to be like?' My mother was pleased at the prospect of the holiday, but some pessimism about one thing or another always had to be thrown in on any project. My father sighed.

'Bert Miles has always known what kind of summer we will have, and what kind of winter we'll have. He's never been wrong. Nobody would take a bet against him on it. He's always right about the weather, says he can sniff it in advance.' My mother made no more challenges, but said she would save to buy all of us some sandals.

Bert Miles was quite right. It was August, the sky was clear, the sun shone and we caught the bus to Stafford. This was the beginning of our first holiday. The war had been over two years, both my parents still continued to work, we now had an electric cooker, a shade over the light bulb, and my mother had purchased two carpets for the front room. Our living standards had greatly improved and now extended to a breath of sea air. Unfortunately for us, standards must have improved for thousands of other people and my father's idea of a holiday was not original to him. The station was crowded with families and suitcases and our platform was the most crowded of all. We managed to squeeze ourselves on to the platform; there was no room for further movement once you had got a position. The train was due at 4.30 in the afternoon. We had already arrived with an hour to spare.

The train arrived half an hour late, it had come from Birmingham, stopped at Wolverhampton and there was not a seat to be seen that was not occupied. Four carriages were more than half empty. I pointed to them.

'First class,' my mother snapped. I didn't understand what she meant.

Along with half of the other would-be travellers we watched our train for Blackpool depart without us. I felt desolate and began to cry.

'Stop that, stop that, we'll get there.' My father could be determined.

'Are we bloody walking it then?' My mother sounded irritable and tired.

My father did not answer her, someone was waving to him, a man further along the platform, almost at the end of it.

'Wait here,' he said. He made his way towards the beckoning arm. There was no announcement over the loud-speaker but the crowds remained where they were. If the train had gone, what were they waiting for? My father returned to us some ten minutes later.

'Follow me.' It was an order. We trailed behind him to the far end of the platform, he carried the sole suitcase and my mother carried a shopping bag; this bag contained food, sandwiches and an orange apiece.

'You know Alf Bates, his Mrs, Elsie, and this is their youngest, Jean.' He gestured to the small family group with one arm as he placed his suitcase to the ground. Alf Bates and his wife greeted my mother with reciprocal nods. Their daughter Jean was younger than me and both of us were too tired to make any acknowledgement of the existence of the other.

'They're going to Blackpool as well,' my father still sounded quite decided.

'Oh ah, and how are we all going to get there?' my mother asked blankly.

'There's a train due at seven, a night train. It takes longer — but it's goin' to Blackpool,' said my father.

'It's right, I've talked to the porter about it. Comes in at seven and we'll be on it.' Alf Bates sounded completely assured. Both women looked at one another and then glanced towards their husbands as though they were re-stating a marriage vow. The looks they gave were an investment of faith. I couldn't believe that we could get on the next train, the platform was still crowded and I was sure that it would be a repeat performance of what had gone before. I sat on the suitcase and stared at the railway lines. I'd never been on a train and it didn't look as though I was about to go on one, whatever the adults said: that's how I felt. Jean Bates must have felt the same because she began to whimper and grizzle very quietly to herself.

'Stop that, stop that our Jean, stop it I tell you. We are going to Blackpool, aren't we Esther?' My mother like Mrs Bates supported her man.

'Yes we are, sit up Tom, stop sulking or I'll give you a crack on the ear. You've heard what yer Dad and Mr Bates have said, so we are having no more nonsense are we Elsie?' Mrs Bates folded her arms to signify agreement. Jean Bates stopped snivelling and I sat up.

It was a long wait. For Jean and me it seemed interminable but the grown-ups seemed to find a new energy from the adversity of the situation. The two women exchanged anecdotes about this woman or that woman whose washing was not white, or whose husband hit her, or just things which meant nothing to me but made them laugh. The men talked about horse racing, football teams, and work at the pit. Then I heard the noise. I heard the train before I saw it. It broke my stupor. I got up from the suitcase — excited, hopeful.

'It's coming Dad. It's coming, I can hear it.'

'Ah, it is, now none of yer move until me and Alf say so. Just stay where you are, take no notice of the rush or the scrambling and fighting that the others get into. That's no way to catch a train.' We were well back from most of the crowd, and I couldn't understand why there were no people near us. The train came into view, steam belching from it, it made hissing and snorting noises as it passed us. It was big and black and the engine had its own smell, I breathed in its fumes as it passed us by. The carriages moved slowly past us, faces were crammed against the corridor windows and no one seemed to be making any attempt at movement within the train. No one was going to get off at Stafford, so how could anyone get on?

The brakes screeched a bit, still the carriages moved, I did not know what to think because all the carriages had moved past us. The two women gave one another puzzled, questioning glances. They too were perturbed. The train came to a halt. There was shouting, even screaming from the rest of the platform where people fought to open doors and squeeze themselves on to the train. It was a horrible sight. A big box-like section of the train pulled up near us. It had no windows and was much taller than the other carriages. Some slide doors clanked open and a porter handed the guard two huge canvas mail bags. He winked at the guard and beckoned my father and Alf Bates forward. They each gave the guard a ten shilling note.

'Jump in quick,' the guard rasped.

My mother and Elsie Bates hopped in swiftly, Mrs Bates jerked Jean aboard with one tug of her arm and my father pushed me in the small of the back. The men followed us in and the sliding doors were shut behind us.

'Where are we dad?' I asked.

'We're in the guard's van, we're on the train, and we're going to Blackpool. So now we make ourselves comfortable, we've more space than anybody else on this train.' We sat on top of great piles of canvas mail bags, we could stretch our legs out, and even lie back if we wanted to, there were no windows so I couldn't see outside. The train began to make loud noises. A shrill whistle penetrated the room, the guard hung from a small door at the back of the van and waved his arm. More noise, a grinding sound beneath us, and then I could feel that we were moving.

'We're off, we're off Elsie,' said my mother. I don't think that I had ever seen her looking so happy.

'We stop at Crewe, it's a slow train, it's running late. We won't be in Blackpool before the morning.' The guard lit a cigarette. His information caused no distress we had achieved what had seemed the impossible. What were a few hours here or there? And Mrs Bates, my mother and me were full of admiration for the men who had got us on the train. We didn't say anything though; in any event Jean Bates had already fallen asleep. What could you expect from a little girl?

The rest of us talked in whispers and the two women combined their food supplies to provide us with our supper. It was a leisurely meal. There were different kinds of sandwiches, a home-made cake, a bottle of milk, somehow it remains fixed in my mind as one of the most distinguished meals of my childhood. Could it have been because we were sharing? Or because of the strange dimly-lit environment in which we ate? I won't ever know. After the meal, I lay back amongst the mail-bags; although I could see nothing, I enjoyed my first train ride. The noise of the engine, the clickety-click sounds as we went along, and the slight swaying rhythm of the guard's van took me over. I entered it all and slept.

'Come on Tom, come on, we're here,' my father woke me. Instantly I knew where we were, there was not the usual vagueness or semi-consciousness that one first experiences on awakening from sleep. We left the guard's van quite refreshed, not fatigued or irritable. My mother said she had slept well, and my father that we couldn't have had a better journey. It was 6.30 in the morning, the air was different and after leaving the station, I saw and heard the first sea gulls. They were very big birds, much bigger than I had imagined. It was the piercing shrieking noises they made that astonished me most.

'We can't knock the landlady up at this hour, shall we have a quick look at the sea front first? I can find the way to the digs better from the front, she drew me a little map, see here it is.' He showed us the map that the landlady had drawn which indicated that we should take a road opposite the North Pier in order to find her. My first view of the sea was a shock. I couldn't see the end of it, it just went on and on. It was grey in colour and not blue. I stared.

'What d'you think of that then?' My dad stared out before him, and I was surprised to see that my mother had linked her arm with his. I didn't answer him, I descended the stone steps

88

of the promenade and stood on the sandy beach. I carved out my name in the sand using the heel of my shoe. I spelled it out in huge letters, as if to let the sea know that I had arrived.

The exercise took up my concentration and attention. When I eventually glanced back towards my parents, I was even more surprised than I had been on seeing the sea. The two of them were clasped in an embrace. My father was kissing my mother on the lips and they seemed to be holding on to the kiss for a long time. I had never seen them do that before. Perhaps the sea had affected them both, I looked down at the sand again. There were some things even a child would not interrupt.

'All the people here are from the Black Country, I have a family from Bilston, a young couple from Wolverhampton, and three youths from West Bromwich. So you see you'll be with all your own folk.' The landlady greeted us, the Lancashire accent sounded alien to me. Mrs Badger had a warm friendly smile and seemed genuinely pleased to see us.

'I'll get you some breakfast after I have shown you your rooms and where the bathroom and toilets are — your son will be sharing a room with the youths from West Bromwich. Better than being on his own and he is a bit on the old side to share a room with you.' Before she could show us up the stairs my father handed her a wad of pound notes.

'I like to get things paid off, never been in debt. You'll find the week's board there missus.' Mrs Badger took the money respectfully and said that she thought in the same way as my father. He spoke to her as she led us through the hallway.

'Oh, we're not from the Black Country, no missus, we're not. We're from Cannock. Cannock Chase, there's lovely countryside around us.' He would always defend his birthplace, if he were in it — or away from it, for him there was no place better. Mrs Badger replied that she didn't know that part of the world too well. Who did, except us?

I had never realised what an active man my father was, nothing was done in leisurely style. Straight after breakfast we were looking at the tower, peering at the fish in the Aquarium. We walked right to the end of the Central Pier. He had booked us in a theatre every single night of our stay. My mother called a halt to the pace and we sat on deck-chairs on one of the piers and enjoyed the sun. I kept looking through the spaces between the slats of wood, watching the tides and currents swirl this way and that. My father went through our future evenings by holding a finger up each time he announced what was in store for us.

'On Monday night, it's Variety, we'll see Dorothy Squires at the Grand Theatre. She's got a good strong voice, her husband's the pianist yer know, and he writes the songs. On Tuesday we're going to the circus at the Tower, famous throughout the world Blackpool Tower Circus is — did yer know that?' He did not expect an answer, but held up a third finger.

'On Wednesday, it's George Formby at The Opera House, they say it's a spectackler show. On Thursday we're seeing the show here on the Pier, it's Donald Peers.'

'Oh, I like him,' said my mother.

'And Friday we are watching a play. Not listening to one our Tom, like you listen to *Saturday Night Theatre* on the wireless, but watching one, with real live actresses and actors.'

'Do we want to watch a play?' my mother asked him. I realised he had booked this one specially for me. His answer was clever.

'It's Wilfred Pickles, you know, *Have a Go* on the wireless. Well, he's in a play. *Hobson's Choice*, that's the name of the play. It's a comedy.'

'That means it's funny,' I said.

'We know what it means thanks, when we don't we'll ask.' My mother was not sharp but she did have an aversion to me if I chose to display any particular intelligence or knowledge that she thought was beyond my age.

Mrs Badger was not stingy with her food. The meals were enormous and well prepared, everyone complimented her. She genuinely liked to please her boarders but there were rules to the house. They didn't affect my dad, my mam or me. The youths from West Bromwich were downcast when these rules were gently but firmly stated before lunch.

'So I'd like you here prompt for meals and as I've already said, the door's locked at half-past eleven. Better safe than sorry I say, and we can't be too careful. I'm sure none of you will be wanting to be out after that time anyway.' The youths looked stricken but on the first night they did get back with about three minutes to spare before the deadline was reached. I pretended to be asleep when they entered the room.

'Eree Tich, you awake?' one of them called out. I was, so there was no point in pretending. I sat up to answer his question. I did not like being called Tich, I wasn't a midget, I was average size for my age. I looked at the one who had called out but he was oblivious to my feelings. This was fair enough as my nick-name had not been delivered with any unkindness.

'Want to earn some money?' another one half whispered. I nodded.

'Well, it's easy see, dead easy. All you have to do is to keep awake until after Mrs Badger's gone to bed. Then just creep downstairs and unbolt the door for us. We want to stay out later — dancing and all that, yer know?'

'Go on Tich, we know you're a sport,' a second youth cajoled. I wasn't that much of a sport — but I was interested, I looked at the three of them. Nothing special to look at, or exciting about any one of them, except that the one who did most of the talking was smaller than the other two and he had blonde almost white hair. His eyebrows were so pale that you could hardly distinguish them.

'How much?' I asked.

'Yer what?' the blonde replied.

'How much will you pay me for doing it, for seeing to the door.' I think they had expected me to do it for nothing, just for the thrill or the naughtiness of the action. They had mentioned payment, not me, so that I didn't feel bad about asking.

'Say half-a-crown?' the blonde suggested the fee.

'Each night I do it, I want half a crown,' I said.

'Bloody 'ell!' one of them exclaimed.

'Oh Billy, it aye much between us; divide it by three and it aye much more than coppers. All right then our ked, yer in business tomorrow. Yer won't forget?' The blonde was the ruler of the group despite his stature. I shook my head and the contract was complete.

Mrs Badger, as well as being kind, was a discreet lady. We had been to the theatre; Dorothy Squire's singing had made my mother cry. This meant that my mother had enjoyed the performance. My parents had taken a drink at a pub near the boarding house and left me to return alone. They arrived back not less than half an hour after me. We had said goodnight to Mrs Badger and gone to our rooms. I sat up in bed reading a Rider Haggard book. There was a tap on the door. I ignored it. The tap was repeated and Mrs Badger called 'All in lads? Are you all in?' Her discretion prevented her from entering and checking.

'Yes, thank you, goodnight,' I called out, not moving from my bed. I heard her ascending the stairs, I assumed that she slept on the top floor in the attic. I read for an hour, perhaps more, then crept downstairs and quickly unbolted the door. I experienced no guilt.

Their talking awakened me, on the third night they talked and whispered longer than they had done on the previous nights. It was impossible to sleep so I listened. It was the blonde who was narrating.

'She's from Redcar. That's in Yorkshire yer know. Anyway, after the last waltz at the Tower Ballroom, I knew there was something in it for me. I dunno how we got around the floor, I'd got my arms all round her, and she had herself up to me real close. I had a hard on up to my neck-hole. It's a wonder I didn't lift her off the floor with it. Anyway, after I saw her home and we went under the pier on the sands. I was everywhere up top with her, and I got her draws off. Had my hand on it and me fingers inside. I'm seeing her again tomorrow and I hope she knows what she's in for.'

The others discussed their exploits but they never matched up to his. His accounts got more vivid as the days went by, what he did to that girl defied all sexual description. I was half expecting him to say that he had eaten her at times. None of the stories shocked me or excited me, mainly because I was sure that they were telling lies. All of them; and what's more I think that they all knew they were, it seemed very important for them to discuss these achievements, but really I thought that they would have been lucky even to get a dance out of a girl, let alone anything else.

'You asleep Tich?' one of them would call out.

'No!'

'Well plug your ears then, you're too young to be listening,' then they would laugh. They paid me the half crown without fail, yet they seemed quite happy about cheating themselves in this way. I think Mrs Badger knew about the arrangement, but she was a sensible woman and never brought the issue up.

With my extra money, I bought presents for my mam and dad. This was something that I had never been able to do before. My mother always kept the plaster-cast clown, he held his upturned pointed cap in his left hand and she used to place pencils, drawing pins, stamps and things like that in it. Blackpool made my mother look prettier, she always had her teeth in and her hair was often covered by an assortment of different patterned head scarves. My father too looked better, the white-grey look had left his face and he was brown and quite handsome. I noticed then that his eyes were green; mine were brown the same as my mother's.

It was a time when we could all really look at one another. I hadn't known the colour of their eyes before then, I'd never spent so much time with them together. It was just one week, only seven days, but I had glimpsed parts of my family that the war had taken away from me. There had been much more effort than just fighting in other countries, and from this time on I was less grudging with regard to my mother's moods. But a week wasn't long enough to allow either of us to get close enough. It was, and remains, a sweet interlude. I think she might even have held my hand during that period.

13
The Newt

'Hold it up, hold the jar up, then we can see their bellies. Oh, they are lovely, nothing I know is as pretty. And the way they just hang in the water like that, so that you can see underneath them. They're not flapping their fins or anything. I wonder how they can just hang like that in the water, without moving anything? In the pond you can only see their backs. I don't think they mind being in the jar for a bit, do you think they like being looked at? The ones with the big tails have stripes running down the sides — can you see? Are they the same as the ones that are yellow on top? They can't be because they're always black, the ones with the big tails. They're crested newts you know.' If Barbara Williams had known the difference between the two varieties of newts then why ask me in the first place? She was a bit of a show-off and if you want to let somebody know that you know something, the easiest way of doing it is to ask a question and then answer it yourself. Barbara Williams did this quite a lot, she was clever about all sorts of things. I liked her.

Most boys did, there was nothing threatening about her in that if you mentioned anything to do with knickers or that sort of thing she would clout you. If you went out anywhere with Barbara, or played with her, it was equal terms and no mysteries with regard to sexual difference. She had the beginnings of tits but you daren't mention them; not that she wanted to be a boy, it was just that she was going to choose all about that when she was ready. Her sense of wonder in most other things was far greater than mine. It was considered babyish to go off on a jaunt with Barbara, the two of us had cycled to Brindley's Brook. It was her idea. It was a two mile trip, the furthest that I had ever cycled. I would never have gone that far without her encouragement.

The new Hudson Bicycle had been in my possession for six weeks or more. My mother had bought it for me and I had felt very badly about my early attempts to ride it. They were poor; it got to a point that after a fortnight of daily help from my father I still lurched and fell to the left or the right, and I wondered whether it was really possible to pedal, travel, move and stay on the mechanism. Unless my father reminded me, I would pretend to forget the evening practice. I wanted to forget the bicycle, give up, walk everywhere as I had done before. My awkwardness filled me with shame.

Barbara Williams put a stop to all that. As I've said, she could do most things, her bicycle was being mended, the front wheel was badly buckled after she had made an over-adventurous curb-stone mounting operation. She saw me pushing my bike up and down the street, me keeping one foot on the pedal and just using it like a scooter as though I were five or six and not nearly eleven.

'Get on the cross-bar and I'll ride it. Stick your legs out, if you catch them in the wheel we'll come off it. You're not scared are you?' She knew that I was.

'Girls' bikes don't have cross-bars,' this was the only defence I could muster to her proposition. It was a lame one, she didn't waste any time.

'I can ride my dad's, his has a cross-bar. I'd be on it now only he needs it for going to work.'

We fell off it three or four times, mainly when she turned corners, but she was firm and at the end of the week I could ride the bicycle with her on the cross-bar. I was grateful and showed it by accompanying her on outings. We took turns on who was passenger. With a boy this might have led to quarrels but not with her. We even took it in turns each day as to the length and type of destination. The newts were her idea. She knew a lot about them, where they were, how they spawned, what they looked like, what they ate . . . so when Brindley's Brook was the choice of the day, I was quite happy to go. Her sense of wonder was infectious, even with regard to newts.

This was how we ended up at Brindley's Brook. You could call it a brook, but it was just an old pit excavation that had filled with water. At its side was a huge great derelict slag heap. This heap of clay and shale had been left a long time, so long that it had become no longer ugly. Like very, very old people, like Mrs Shirley who was full of lines but comfortable and — yes, pretty. The slag heap was decorated with tufts of elephant grass, colts-foot, and willow herb. Barbara said it was a small grey, yellow, green and pink mountain. She often talked like that. Some kids couldn't stand her, particularly when she was sounding off in that way, as far as I was concerned it was like being with a picture book. She saw things the same as me, oniy she always managed to see more even if we were looking at the same things.

At the other side of the pool ran the railway. And here on the sidings there grew blackberries, but Barbara also found a tree with small yellow plums on it.

'They're greengages, don't tell anyone. If you do they won't believe you. Nobody will believe there would be green-gage trees growing on a railway siding. But don't tell anyone or they'll pick them before they're ripe. We'll come back and get them later in the year.' And she meant it.

I parted the green algae slowly with my hands and saw another newt in the water. Yellow-backed, motionless. My

97

hands were cupped together in readiness to move slowly beneath him, levering him from the water without him being aware of it. They were like that, sometimes you might think they were half asleep when you caught them in this gentle fashion. They hardly stirred until you transferred them into the jar. Barbara said she had taught herself to catch them in this way. You never grabbed at a newt. My hands were underneath him. He was mine.

'We don't need any more Tom,' she called from the bank. I was surprised. Whether we needed any more or not it was unlike her to intervene when the operation had got to such a delicate stage. I half turned, the newt sensed the tremor in the water as my hands moved, and drifted away to disappear into some weeds.

Barbara sat on the bank. She was no longer peering into the jar. Her eyes were directed towards the road, where the bicycle was leant against a small bridge which allowed a trickle of water to go beneath the road and reappear on the other side. A man in an RAF uniform was leaning on the bridge and looking towards us. Barbara looked back at him, she looked at him like she stared at the bellies of the newts. But her face was not alive in the same way, she was frowning.

'I think we should walk back to the road,' she said. She got up without waiting for me to agree, she left the newts there on the bank in the jar. I followed her and as she walked, she stumbled a bit. This was because she wasn't picking her way carefully along the shale bank. She couldn't, as her eyes never left the man, she stared at him as we got nearer. I felt uncomfortable because she had gone quiet.

Ten yards, we couldn't have been much further than that from him. 'Leave it; take yer bloody hands off it,' Barbara screamed. It was a high pitched shriek that came from her, as though she had known what he was about to do but had been forced to bottle up the knowledge for too long. 'Oh, you sod, you bugger. . . .' she ran towards him. I remained still, immobilised by his action. He had seized the handlebars

98

of the bicycle and leapt astride the saddle, the bike had begun to move. Barbara had caught up with him, she grabbed the rough blue serge cloth of his jacket and pulled at him from behind. The bike had gone a little forward but was halted. I ran towards them, but before I reached the two of them he seized her hair, jerked her head backwards and flung her on to the curbside.

She was on her feet by the time that I reached her and he was pedalling away. On my bike — our bike.

'Quick, after him,' she gasped. We both raced behind him, shouting foul words at the thief who increased his distance from us with every stride that we took. Like a bad dream, our legs could not keep up with the chase. They would not move fast enough, as in a dream our thighs seemed weighted. He glanced over his shoulder as he passed under the railway bridge. Barbara had still not given up, she was ahead of me now. Shock and bewilderment dawned inside of me, my legs moved more slowly — yet I was not breathless.

A train had paused on the top of the railway bridge. Carriageless, it let only a trickle of steam belch from its side. The engine driver leaned from his train. He had had a clear view of the proceedings, he was isolated. He couldn't leave his train. He shouted an obscenity at the RAF man. And then, our desperation seemed to be contagious. Huge lumps of coal were being hurled from the engine down at the road. They fell like ammunition, but none found their mark. We stopped running, the road was littered with shattered pieces of coal. My bike was gone. Barbara picked at a piece of the debris. Then she took a lump of coal in her hand and threw it at the empty roadway, when it hit the ground I began to cry. Shock had passed and I was now racked with grief. I slumped and sat on the kerb. It was some time before I could speak. All this time, she stood with her arm about me, interspersing swear words and curses with condolence. I was sad, but she was angry.

'My mam will kill me — I'll get a good hiding,' my voice

had returned, Barbara did not add any more words to my thin wail. She took my hand, held on to it all the way home (she was one of the few girls that could do this and not think that anyone would say anything about her; they didn't, they wouldn't dare).

'It wasn't Tom's fault, Mrs Wakefield. Honest it wasn't.' Barbara had gone through the events of the afternoon, her account was clearly documented, detailed and unsentimental. My mother lit a cigarette. Barbara did not leave the living room but remained at my side.

'He's not getting a good hiding, is he?' Barbara asked. My mother blew a cloud of smoke into the air.

'He must have been running away from something. Perhaps his National Service upset him. It don't suit all the young men, it's a bit different if there is a war on.'

'Yer what, Mrs Wakefield?' Barbara was astonished with my mother's calm, as I was.

'The man who took Tom's bike,' she replied. At the mention of my bicycle I began to cry again — quietly.

'Stop that now, shut up. I'll save, I've saved before, I'll save and buy you another one. Go out and play now. Go and play with Barbara.' She looked worn and stood from her chair, indicating that she wanted to be alone. She wasn't angry or upset, the news had just made her look more tired.

'You mam is nice, she is you know.' Barbara was insistent. She forced me to nod my head in agreement with her. As I say, Barbara could see things better, see things differently; possibly I couldn't see my own mother as well as she could see her. I was surprised when Barbara led me back to Brindley's Brook. At this point of the day I would have followed her anywhere. I didn't want to catch any more newts. Neither did she.

'You had forgotten about them, hadn't you?' Barbara held up the jar and peered at the newts.

'Yes,' I was no longer interested.

'If we had left them they'd have died. It would have been

our fault,' she said. She poured the contents of the jar, water, a spray of weed, newts and all, on to the bank near the water's edge. We watched the newts make slow but deliberate progress towards their natural home. They would pause occasionally, and look about them, as if they couldn't believe their good luck. Only one remained on the bank, a large one, with a black back and a crested tail.

Barbara watched him, he had come to a complete standstill. He didn't seem to care whether he entered the water or not. Perhaps he was exhausted, stricken, or just bored.

'If that man, the RAF man who took your bike — if that man had been a newt, I would have slit his belly open.' This imagery of Barbara's startled me, after all, she loved newts, particularly their spotted bellies. I was afraid for the creature who still remained dormant, unaware of her thoughts.

She picked up the long-tailed newt with the greatest of care, she let it crawl a little on the palm of her hand. Then with great tenderness she let him glide and slip off her hand as she lowered him gently into the water. 'There,' she said. 'There, there, join your mates.'

14

The Anniversary

If Sundays were anything to go by, then most of our neighbours must have thought me a most dutiful and devout boy. Mrs Archer would smile at me from her front gate, a nice friendly woman, always gentle, always smiling. She would watch me, dressed in my best suit on a Sunday afternoon, as I passed by her house. 'Off to church then Tommy?' She knew I would say yes and would nod approvingly. On Sundays I went to church both in the afternoon and in the evening. As far as I could gather from my parents (both of whom seemed totally indifferent to religion), I had been christened C. of E., but they were very vague about this and I really wondered whether or not I had been christened at all. This did not worry me as I thought that I could change my first name more easily when I got older. At that time I would have preferred to be called 'Tony', but was stuck with 'Tom'.

In spite of my foggy Anglican heritage, I chose to attend non-conformist places of worship. From January until June I attended the Primitive Methodist Church, and from the middle of June until the end of December I changed the pace and went to the Bethany Baptist Chapel. My reasons for doing this were not due to any changing doubts as to the interpretation and delivery of Christianity. The whole method of change was brought about by the 'Star Card'. Each visit to the Church or Chapel was documented by this card being stamped. If your attendance or number of visits were above a certain total, then you were entitled to a prize. This was always in the form of a book, not necessarily a religious one, but one about stamp collecting or even one with several adventure yarns in it. Although I was a member of the local library, I could never own books unless I worshipped and praised God. It was possible to score enough stars at each church and own two books, if you got your timing right.

It was the singing which reduced my personal library to one book a year. The Baptist Church announced a date for their anniversary, it was an ambitious project. Sixty children, about forty girls and twenty boys, were enlisted to sing the anniversary anthems. There were ten songs in all, every one of them new to us. We were the most mixed *ad hoc* choir imaginable. Untrained, unmusical, interested in attending only because members of the opposite sex would sometimes smile favours at us. Most of us boys were now aware of girls, we didn't know how to talk to them but it was exciting standing near them on the anniversary platform. Sometimes notes were passed along; one sentence love letters, but there was a genuine passion behind the five words and the stealthy glances. I never sent any notes, there was a girl, her name was unattractive, but she didn't need a glamorous name looking as she did. She had dark brown hair which she wore in two plaits; before now we had always called them pigtails. There was nothing of the look of a pig about her. The hair showed her long white pretty neck. Her brow was free of any fringed hair that was in fashion. A wide brow and large deep blue eyes looked out from a face that I found painfully angelic. She had one verse which she sang solo and we all stared at the pretty lips and were entranced by the thin sweet voice.

Unfortunately for me, several of the other boys were captivated by her; most of these boys were a little older than me. Perhaps it was the solo that helped attract attention to her. She was not a vivacious girl — but she would smile, smile very slowly, sometimes as though she knew about the things that we didn't know about. It was a difficult decision, either seeing her once or twice a week and giving up a book or going to the Methodist Church. The dates were getting close, I had three weeks in which to make my choice.

It did not take any brave overtures on my part, I was rejected before I had even begun. Her affections were already sworn to another boy, it was no secret, everyone knew. He even went to her house for tea. Her father must have been quite rich because I was told that he owned the coal lorry that he drove. And she did not live in a row of houses. There was just her house and another, just the two. Next to her house was a big yard and a large garage for the lorry to back into. I checked on these details and they were all true. I followed the girl and the boy one afternoon, and watched her mother smile and greet her daughter and the boy. It was as though he were related to them. I felt angry and cheated about this.

Now there was still time (with an excuse) to enrol at the Methodist Chapel, and get another book. But we had started practising the songs. I had begun to sing some of them at home; only when I was on my own, though. I continued to attend the Baptist Church, like many of the others I was now grudgingly to begin to respect Jeavon Burton. He was the organist and choir master. Much against all our non-training and prejudice, somehow he had got us to enjoy singing. We never admitted it to him.

On the contrary, some afternoons we were treacherous and unkind. We would sing off key, or not come in at a particular place when the girls had finished off a trill of verses, we would see his hand go up whilst his other hand played the melody on the organ. We would clam up our mouths and wait for his outbursts. 'Altos, come on altos,' that was us, the boys, he called us altos. We often sang the same words as the girls but to a different tune. Sometimes we had bits on our own. 'Altos, altos,' he would shout despairingly. Then he would have to stop playing the organ and stand up and beseech us. This was precisely what we wanted him to do. We could cough and the girls didn't help matters because they encouraged us with titters and giggles. After we had been so nasty to him, do you know what he would do? He'd apologise to us.

'Now lads, I'm sorry I've shouted. I should have run through that with you more carefully before. Take no notice of my temper.' What temper? 'Just come in when I put up my hand, you can mark it in pencil on your hymn sheets if it will help. I know you can do it; it's me that gets too upset too quickly. I shouldn't fly off like I do; come on then lads, let's have it again. I know you can do it. Come on now, please, please.' He would plead in this way. This large, heavy, bold bespectacled man would cajole us in this manner.

Somehow, he always extracted some mercy from us. But we never completed a rehearsal without us doling him out some punishment. At the end of the rehearsals he would thank us all, often attempting to do it individually as we were leaving. He really believed in his worship and he transferred this to us, his choir. He must have done, because we all attended regularly and any pairings between boys and girls had long since been consolidated. If a song went particularly well, his face would lose its frown as he played the organ and transfused with delight, it would take on an entranced relaxed expression. Then, he would stand in front of us all, he could be quite dramatic. He would shake his head from side to side and not speak for a few seconds. 'Well, I don't know, I don't know, if anybody had told me a month ago that I would hear singing like that from you all, I wouldn't have believed it. No, I wouldn't have believed it myself. That was beautiful, no Jack I'm not joking so don't laugh, no choir will ever do it better.' We enjoyed his praise as much as his agony because we knew that he felt and meant both.

It was a shock to see my parents getting dressed in their best clothes after our Sunday lunch. They never attended church of any kind, and I hadn't expected them to attend the anniversary. My mother had kept a clean white shirt for me and gave me strict instructions not to get it dirty as it had to make do for the evening performance as well. 'You had better be going now,' my mother commanded. I looked at them, still unsure as to whether they were going out on a visit or . . . .

'We'll be there, we're coming to hear the singing, I don't like preaching, but a bit of good singing settles yer dinner.' My father straightened his tie in front of the mirror. I left for the chapel.

The place was packed to capacity, with people standing at the back. The audience, at least the size of it, frightened many of us as we stood clean and sparkling on the raised platforms. The tallest at the back and the smallest in the front row. We could all be seen. The congregation whispered a little but we were mute. Jeavon Burton came in from a little door on the left. Sister Bessie made a few welcoming remarks. Then Jeavon walked to the middle of the floor, he faced us, his back was to the audience. He held up his thumb and he winked and smiled. He said nothing.

There were no mistakes. We astonished ourselves. We did achieve something quite beautiful as he had said we would. When it was over, the congregation were smiling, some were crying and money rained into the collection box.

The evening performance was even more crowded, people stood in the aisles as well as at the back of the chapel. There was no applause, just this intense murmur of appreciation as they were leaving which was tantamount to an accolade as the comments were tinged with awe and admiration. I was sorry it had all ended. Jeavon Burton thanked us, he was an emotional man and became quite tearful. Quite overcome with our own efforts, we never thanked him.

It was a surprise to find my parents waiting outside for me. They always attended the Working Men's Club on Sunday evenings, they had attended the anniversary twice and had given up an evening of pleasure which I knew meant a lot to them. It was not in context. I did not understand.

'You heard me, you heard it all this afternoon. Did you want to hear the singing twice?' I asked.

My father gave me a look which denoted that I was ignorant of some vital facts, my mother took his arm and frowned at me. 'Since when did you decide what we do of an evening?' she did not snap, there was mild humour in her question.

'We didn't come to hear you sing tonight. We heard you sing this afternoon.' My father spoke very deliberately. I felt hurt by his remark. What were they dressed up for then? I was bold. I grumbled at them.

'What did you come for then?' I began to walk past them but my mother clawed at my shoulder.

'Your dad's talking to you,' she said with menace. I rejoined them.

'It's like this our Tom, we listened to the singing in the afternoon. But in the evenin' we put our ears to the organ. Nobody plays the organ like Jeavon Burton does; nobody in Britain, so you'd be daft to miss out on a chance of hearing him. And what does he do? He has all you kids singing like you've never sung in your lives before; all for nothing. And him as clever as he is.'

'Jeavon's a good man,' my mother added almost off-handedly.

'Is he a Baptist, mam?' I asked, correlating goodness with the establishment.

'How the hell should I know?' she replied.

15

Out of Season

The previous summer when it had been too cold to swim, I had watched a man fishing. I had only placed my bare foot in the pool to know that it would make my balls ache if I went in the water above my waist. I dressed quickly and sat behind the man on the bank of the pool. He never spoke, he took no notice of me at all, his eyes never left his float. I couldn't understand the fascination, but his stillness and indifference to my presence compelled me to sit still and quiet. There were no ripples on the pool, and the float, red topped, stood upright and erect in the water. I was not going to give in, I stared at it too, I couldn't believe there were any fish swimming around there underneath it. It seemed like hours, then it happened.

The float bobbed, just a little, but it did bob. I wanted to call out to the man. Had he noticed? He had, his neck was craned forward and his head was raised ready to seize the fishing rod from its forked iron resting place. The float began to travel across the pool making little bobs as it did so. I could hardly breathe, I didn't dare move. It bobbed once, twice, three times and then the red tip shot below the surface of the water. He jerked the fishing rod, the end bent over and I watched him reel in the fish. I had forgotten my self-imposed stillness and scrambled to his side to watch him land the fish. He removed the hook from its lip and held it in a wet cloth for me to see. It was silver but had pretty coloured dots running down its side.

'It's a rainbow, a rainbow trout. Not often you get them from the pool, they're mostly in the stream that feeds it.' Horn's Pool was blessed with both a quick running stream and a small waterfall. I stared at the fish. I watched him catch other fish and stayed on into the late afternoon. Captivated by the sport, I itemised and memorised all that he did.

Each Saturday until the end of the summer I watched him, and quietly he taught me the terms. Bait, types of fish, size of hooks, keep nets: I learned all about the rudiments of fishing. We never exchanged names and we never discussed anything else. My behaviour was perfect, I never moved. I watched and listened when I was spoken to; apart from that, tutor and pupil demanded nothing else of each other.

I saved money and bought my own fishing rods and gear that Christmas. I hadn't imagined that you fished in the winter time — so it was a long wait until that first hot day towards the end of May before I set out to fish Horn's Pool for myself. I knew where to collect my bait. Really good bait, that I could glean on my bicycle on the way to the pool. I stopped at the entrance to the pit and pushed my bicycle towards a discarded pile of wooden pit-props. A huge mound of pony manure rose above my head, it looked like pale thatch as the sun had baked its surface dry: I dug into it with a stave of wood, the steam rose, the deeper I dug the more fecund the manure became. There they were, masses of juicy red worms in great clusters. All ready for the afternoon. I filled my bait tin and left a little manure with the worms to keep them fresh. I had enough worms for a fortnight's fishing.

I only needed enough for half a day, that's what I paid

for at the public house which owned the grounds where the pool stood. Threepence for half a day's fishing. The landlord of the pub had changed. When I knocked at his back door, he seemed to be surprised or ignorant. My request seemed to bemuse him.

'Fish? What do you want to fish for?' There really was no answer. I shrugged and held out my threepenny bit. He took it, business must have been poor. 'Mind how you go while you're about that pool, it's deep, as deep as ten feet from some of the banks.' I didn't tell him that I could swim, that I knew the mysteries of the pool. Thanks, false thanks, were smiled in exchange for his information.

It was a surprise to find the pool deserted. A few coots trailed and squawked across its surface, but there were no swimmers, no fishermen, I had the place to myself. I was glad of that. Instead of going to the grass slopes on the further side of the pool where I could sit comfortably and fish in the shallows, I chose the most difficult part of the pool. It was the narrowest section and the waterline was thickly wooded. Here the pool was at its deepest right near the edge. With some difficulty I managed to find a space in the undergrowth of trees, one had fallen, perhaps struck by lightning or its roots had rotted with age. The great trunk of the tree half sprawled between the bank and the pool. By sitting astride the trunk of the fallen tree, I could fish deep, I could cast near or far, and still be in water that might be rampant with fish. My sitting position was not uncomfortable and I could hook my keep-net on to one of the trunk's half-shorn branches so that it sank into the water. Preparation was slow, I wanted no tangled lines, I wanted the float to cock correctly into position, I wanted to begin efficiently. A few worms were scattered into the pool to attract the fish to the spot where I chose to cast my line. Plop! First time the float bobbed into a correct position. I had cast correctly. I was prepared to be patient, prepared for a long wait, prepared for no bites at all. The pool was

110

mine. The sense of ownership was immense, I would have loathed intruders, as for the solitude, I was unaware of it.

Almost immediately the float bobbed and then dived under the water. The shock of this action almost before the line had settled on the water all but caused me to topple off the log and into the pool. I grabbed on to the side with my left hand and jerked the rod with my right. A fish was landed within a minute, a small perch four or five inches long. The large mouth, the strange hump to its back, the dorsal fin, just like the ones on a shark, the blue-green of its back, the dark stripes running from its beautiful back to its silvery belly, all fascinated me. It was the first fish I had ever caught. I freed the hook from its mouth with great care and gently dropped it into the keep-net.

Whilst watching my tutor those few months before, there was always time for contemplation between catching one fish and the rest. At times, the intervals could be an hour or more. This never mattered much. But my first expedition was different; there was barely time for thought. The line would go in and another small perch would come out. All I could think was that those fish were bloody starving or that a shoal had settled right where I had chosen to fish. In the space of two hours there must have been thirty or more fish in the keep-net. I had missed some of them too, much too eager I had snatched at the rod too quickly and thus given six or seven fish temporary freedom. My arm had begun to ache and I was feeling a little disgruntled in that none of the fish exceeded six inches. I knew perch could be much larger. Time to change tactics perhaps, bide my time and hope for bigger and better things, quality not quantity for a change.

'The big ones are near the bottom, sometimes on it,' he had said more than once. I decided to fish deeper, I cast my line close near the end of the log and the float indicated that the bait was just touching the bottom of the ten foot depth. This time it remained still and I waited. It seemed a long time, but I was sure there was a large fish there.

111

I stretched back on the long tree trunk and lay sprawled, my head cupped between my hands. The rod was left unattended, balanced between the trunk of the tree and some convenient twigs. It was pleasant just to lie there like that and just rest and hope. My eyes never left the float, I knew it would happen.

It did. From a flat position the float perked and stood bolt upright, before I could get into a sitting position it had gone under the water, the end of my rod was pulled from its twig mooring. I grasped the handle of the rod. This was all that was necessary, that large perch had hooked itself. It was just a question of swinging it towards me, the line was not more than five feet from me and I moved as swiftly as I could. If I gave the fish more time, I knew that the line would snap. I was not skilled in the art of 'playing' a fish. It was heavy, its green and silver body swerved towards me and I clutched at it with my free hand. A searing pain almost made me release the fish. Its fin was spiked, it was like grasping four or five needles. What a strange fish it was; not eight inches, but so heavy, so fat. Nervous with excitement one of my feet slipped into the water. I ignored the mishap.

'Careful how you handle that fish, better let me do it, that is not ready to come out of the water.' Startled, I turned, still holding on to the fish. It was him, my tutor. I don't know how long he had been watching me. He had no fishing gear with him and he was making his way along the tree trunk towards me. I had never interfered with his fishing.

'I can manage,' I said, hoping to stop him in his tracks. He continued to edge gingerly along the tree trunk.

'Ah, I daresay you can, but I was thinking of the fish. It's in no condition to be mauled about.' He took the rod from me, he had wet his handkerchief in the pool and placed the fish carefully encased in the sodden cloth. He unhooked it with great tenderness and then placed it back in the water. Strange, the fish seemed to pause on the surface before

112

making a cumbersome dart to the left until it finally swam into the depths out of sight.

'That was the biggest, it was the biggest of them all!' I cried out to him bitterly. He looked at me with some pity and glanced towards my keep net.

'Caught many then lad?'

'Plenty, stacks of them, stacks of perch. All the others are small, that was the biggest,' I said.

'Only its belly lad, only its belly. It's spawning. They're all spawning now. You shouldn't be fishing. The season is closed. It's not your fault, that silly bugger at the pub should have told yer. He don't love fish like you and me.'

'Closed?' I didn't understand.

'Ah yes, this is the time they have their young. That was a heavy mother you had on your line. If she had died, you'd have killed fifty perch, perhaps more. You wouldn't want to do that, would yer now?'

'I didn't know.'

'Course yer didn't. Best pack up your things and wait till the season starts proper.' I obeyed him and emptied the small perch back into the water.

'We can look for crayfish if you like.' He was a kind man and we footled about the rocks at the bottom of the water-fall. We found two crayfish and we even let them go, after we had looked at them.

'It would have been murder, wouldn't it, I mean if I had banged that fish's belly?' I was about to leave him and was sitting astride my bicycle.

'Abortion, abortion maybe but not murder lad. I'll see you when the season opens. Ter-ra.'

'Ter-ra,' I called after him.

'Catch any?' my father asked when I arrived home.

'Only cray fish,' I lied.

'Crayfish!' my mother exclaimed.

'They're like little lobsters, only they're in fresh water, not in the sea.'

113

'I've never heard of anybody going fishing for them,' she said.

'Gypsies do, and they eat hedgehogs.' My father laughed when I answered.

'You're no gypsy our Tom, what do you want doing catching those horrible things for?'

'Oh, dad, you should know it's the "closed season", you can't fish for ordinary fish now. If you do, they'll have abortions.' I must have sounded superior, I liked using new words on them.

'Who have you been talking to?' my mother asked.

'Nobody.'

'Where did you hear that word?'

'I've known what it meant, but not the word,' I said.

She shook her head slowly, looked at my father and said, 'You see Dick, he's old-headed, much too old-headed.'

'Forget it then, forget that word,' he said.

I nodded to please them, but how can you forget a word when you know what it means?

16

Fancy Dress

The perfume was very heavy, I sniffed deeply, loving its heady effect upon me; Ann Dando, who was the licensee of the Star and Garter, sloshed it about her throat, neck, armpits and bosom in generous fashion. The perfume was called 'June' and as if to emphasise the quality of the fragrance and the amount of well-being it could convey, she dabbed some on her son Colin and some on me.

'There duck, just a bit on your foreheads, sip your port and lemon, it's good for your blood. Finish off the sandwiches, it's best ham; off the bone. Don't tell yer mam I'm giving you port and lemon or she'll be after me. You can tell yer dad, he won't mind. How is he?' She always asked after my father, Colin said they should get together, his mother and my father; he said it would be good for them both. His mother must have conveyed this worldly opinion to him; she made no bones about her affection for my dad. 'He's a lovely little man, I could bloody eat him,' she would say this sort of thing to me. I hadn't thought of my dad as little, but compared to Ann Dando, I suppose he was.

Whereas my father could have been considered as slightly

below average height for a man, Ann Dando was most certainly tall for a woman, six foot perhaps. If she had been of bean-stalk proportions she would not have been attractive, but she was blessed with an ample bosom and quite a sizeable behind. Men would refer to her as a 'big' woman. This was meant as a compliment, her size matched the comfort of her outlook. Like some large settee, you could rest on Ann, she would absorb and comfort, she was both fixed and yielding. Perhaps the only person that I had ever met who appeared to be entirely without prejudice. She treated Colin and me like Gainsborough's paintings of children — the children were dressed like adults — Ann communicated with us as if we were miniature adults. No secrets, not on any issue.

'Minnie will probably be a bit late this morning, had too much dick last night. A bit of dick will keep any woman lying in late, it can happen in the morning.'

'Mother!' Colin exclaimed pretending to be shocked. She threw her head back and laughed at his reaction, her long earrings shook as she chortled.

'I'm not that bad am I Tommy? Only saying what others think, don't you tell yer mam though.' I wouldn't have dreamt of telling my mother; odd, I don't think my mother would have cared very much about Ann's somewhat vulgar observations. Like many people who could be termed vulgar (by prigs or bigots) she was extraordinarily tender and original. What other woman would ply two boys with port and lemon before eleven in the morning?

'Oh, Tommy, you do look nice today. When you're older you'll be handsome; not as handsome as our Colin though. I can't believe he'll ever get old.'

'I won't grow old,' said Colin. This sounded daft to me. Everybody did (yet both their predictions proved correct, in later years he was drowned whilst touring with a repertory company in Australia. He was twenty-two years old).

'Oh, our Colin, why can't you go as something beautiful,

I mean couldn't you both go as something from the Arabian Nights? I could put cocoa on your faces and you could borrow my earrings, the dressing up box is full of . . . . '

'No, if we go looking too smart we won't win. We have to look ordinary and ugly,' he replied. I made no contribution, as long as we collected some prize money from the Fancy Dress Parade I really didn't care what I looked like. Colin held up a large sheet of white card. It announced our roles for the forthcoming afternoon, 'Pram-Girl with Baby'.

'But duck, my darlin', there's hundreds of women with prams. That's what happens when a war ends. Couples settle down to it. You'll look like everybody else in the park.'

'Not if I'm six times as big as you are — I'm going to be big; big at the front and big at the back. We'll win,' he answered her, cool and confident. I thought of the £5 prize.

'What about me?' I asked. I couldn't see where I was to fit into the arrangements.

'You're in the pram. You're the baby,' he said. He must have noticed my expression. I felt crestfallen; I couldn't see how me being a baby could possibly impress the judges.

'It's easy for you, all you have to do is suck at your bottle and shake your rattle, we've got a bonnet and a night shirt. Me mam will powder your face. Leave the rest to me. We've borrowed one of those prams with high wheels, so don't tip it over, just do as you're told. Like babies ought to. I have to get ready; Mother you can give us a hand, only if I tell you.' His manner was often imperative, even as a child he seemed in total control of his daily destiny. This included mine. It took him nearly two hours to get ready — I was prepared in ten minutes. What a strange way to celebrate an election. The 1945 election was a celebration, I didn't know quite why, everybody seemed to be voting Labour. My parents had refused again and again to tell me what party they were voting for. I asked Ann about her political affiliations as she smothered my face with powder.

'Oh, I vote with the customers darlin', it's Labour this

117

time, oh yes, I vote with the customers.' That summarised her political thought but left me bewildered.

She helped me into the pram; I could just squeeze into it, my knees stuck in the air. I was not comfortable but any thoughts of comfort had to be sacrificed on the altar of art and prize money. She fixed a canopy over the pram. The July day was warm and sunny.

'There, that will keep the sun off yer head; let me just tie your bonnet tight. We don't want it slipping off.' She had begun to talk to me like people do talk to babies. All clucking noises and little sense. If I had the bonnet on, why put the pink fringed canopy over me? Like a baby, I whimpered an incoherent response. Then Colin appeared.

'Good God, our Coll,' his mother exclaimed. I dropped the rattle — shocked by the apparition.

'Don't drop it again; mother, pick it up please. I can't bend down,' he was quite serious.

'Oh our Colin, how could you? I've never seen anything like it in all my life,' she then broke into heavy laughter, tears streamed from her eyes and she held her sides as she rocked with mirth. I joined her, but he put a stop to it.

'You're not allowed to laugh, other people can but not you. You can glug, gurgle or cry. If you laugh we won't win first prize.' I obeyed. Ann continued, having to wipe her eyes and recover her emotions several times before she was eventually ready to help launch us both into the street. I had to avert my eyes from him. If I had a mother looking like he did, I would have chosen to have travelled totally unaccompanied from birth.

Her breasts stood out at least three feet from her body, the arse seemed so wide and so low slung that it almost resembled a trailer on a lorry — an addendum that one had to haul. She had an acid-yellow and red headscarf done up in turban style. Big drop earrings hung from her ear lobes, one was yellow and one was red. A red mouth of enormous proportions had been painted on to the face and the eyebrows

118

curved over and round and ended midway on her cheek bones. Colin (like his mother) was tall, a pair of high-heeled shoes shot him up even higher. Like some grotesque giantess from a fairy tale, he ambled over and pushed me back further into the pram. I was relieved to see that he could walk. His mother saw us to the roadway.

'How did yer get your titties that size?' she asked him.

'Socks and balloons.'

'Oh, dear God,' she started to laugh again, then stopped. 'How are you going to get there? The park is a good mile's walk. You'll fall to bits our Colin, before you get there.'

'Not if he keeps still in the pram. If we're left alone, we'll get to the park in one piece,' he called over his shoulder and had already begun to push me and the pram up the hill.

We did get there. Nobody hindered us, some people called out after us but there were other things to be witnessed besides us. We had joined in the parade. There were children's tap groups, other fancy dress competitions, decorated coal lorries with characters in tableau on the back of them. Much to Colin's irritation we were not entirely the centre of attraction.

Deservedly, some of the coal lorries brought 'oohs' and 'ahs' from the crowds. These once dirty utilitarian vehicles were now transformed into transient moving works of art. The miners or their wives responsible for arranging and decorating these machines showed that they were not void (if given the chance) of creating something quite special. It was the swan that impressed me the most. The lorry had been covered with small pieces of white crêpe paper. Each piece of paper must have been individually curled, the lorry was covered with them. It gave the effect of being coated with feathers. Somehow the sides of the lorry had been extended upwards to resemble wings. The bonnet of the lorry was a suitably orange beak. This great bird carried seven or eight teenage girls, all dressed in white and gold. The girls sat quite still as the crowds gazed in admiration; how it affected

119

the girls is difficult to know — but when would they ever travel on the back of a swan again? Colin said that they looked soppy, but nevertheless I wondered if he would have liked to have exchanged his incongruous role for their enchanting one. But incongruous we had both chosen to be, we were stuck with it and forced to play our parts through to the end.

Cannock Park was crowded, it was more of a carnival and a celebration than a political meeting. Several platforms were dotted about the huge meadow which stretched from the tiny cricket pavilion for acres all around. Just open grassland, perfect for the gathering. A voice boomed over the loudspeaker and announced a speaker — 'Miss Jenny Lee'. She stood on one of the platforms. The first politician I had ever seen. Colin pushed the pram forward through the crowds so that we could have a closer look at her. She didn't look like any of the women that I had seen in Cannock. She wore a shiny black dress with a red rose pinned on to it, she spoke without notes, her voice was loud but clear, a Scots accent added a new dimension. What is more, she was very beautiful, the nearest I had ever seen to what a film star might look like. Colin and me couldn't understand what she was saying but joined in the applause when she had finished speaking as though we had witnessed a performance of grandeur rather than a political speech. Her presence had held our attention and momentarily all thoughts of our physical discomforts were forgotten.

The rest of the Fancy Dress candidates were more organised than we were. Most of the children taking part were accompanied by their parents and the majority of the contestants were girls with mothers who kept adding bits on to them or straightening out frills. There were girl Bo-peeps carrying lambs, girl-poodles, endless girl-fairies, girl-Jack-Frosts covered in white glitter. They were all beautifully turned out. Two boys had both chosen to be Charlie Chaplin and clearly hated the sight of one another. Colin said that as there were

120

two of them, neither of them had a chance of winning. This revitalised his assurance which had begun to sag during the heat of the afternoon.

We were instructed to parade around in a circle whilst the judges scrutinised us. The selection was by elimination. If you received a tap on the shoulder, then you were out. You left the circle. The judges had a gentle steward who was responsible for this irksome and painful task. The competitors trailed around dreading the pending tap of death on their shoulder, they moved silently — self-conscious. Not Colin, no one had said that the competitors were to remain mute. From the second we began, he called out at the crowds. They called back at him and their responses fed his histrionics and increased his comic fervour.

'This is my sixteenth, missus,' (he pointed at me) 'I never get a rest. My old man is better than Charles Atlas.'

'My husband's not big yer know. I make do for both of us. Yes, he's got plenty to get hold of!'

'Oh, missus, I had a horrible time with this one, thought I was having quads. They had to get a truck to load me into the ambulance.'

'Yes, darlin', it was like carrying a ton of coal, the size of him. It took two doctors to smack his arse when he was born. One held him and the other one slapped. Yes, he bit them. First thing he did when he opened his mouth.'

'It's me hips, me hips, I reckon I could have eight at a time but my husband's not up to it. He's always tired, says he works night and day, says I wear him out. Look at me — would I wear anybody out?'

I just sucked at the bottle and screamed out when Colin hissed at me to do so. Our shoulders were not tapped, there seemed more space in the circle. There were only three contestants left. A cute little fairy was handed a piece of card which said '3rd' and was tapped. Then it happened, we were tapped; Colin was half way through some cat-call when he received the tap and was given the '2nd' card. He spoke to the usher very quietly, I felt sick.

'You must have made a mistake.' The man shook his head.

'No — second prize — three pounds.'

We stood on the platform, we were clapped, we received our prize money. Colin did not speak again. The crowd were entitled to no more fun at our expense. The second position did not satisfy him. As soon as we had received our money, he said that we should go straight home. This was more difficult than we had imagined. Getting into the park had been simple but tough on his feet, his mother's shoes had given him blisters, yet we had not been hindered by the onlookers. As entertainers we were given an access, a certain social leeway and licence. We were part of the show and respect had been proffered. Now the show was over.

A gang of youths needed some target practice. We were the most obvious candidates. They had surrounded us before we reached the park gates. We tried to barge past them, Colin bashed them with the pram if they blocked our way. One of them seized the baby's bottle and squirted milk into my face. Colin snatched it off him and I leapt out of the pram. We began to run as quickly as we could. This was not very fast. His shoes were not designed for running and small gravel stones bit into my bare feet. They pulled at Colin's clothing so that bits and pieces of clothing were torn away from their pin-holds. There was a loud bang. I watched Colin's left breast shrink and disappear as one of the youths stabbed his lighted cigarette into it. Half of Colin's arse shrivelled up when they attacked rear-guard fashion.

At this point, he stepped out of his mother's shoes. Picked them up and handed one to me. We stood behind the pram.

'You come any closer you buggers and you'll get this in your eyes,' he waved the spike heel of the shoe in their faces. I held up my shoe ready to do just what Colin had indicated if the tor-ment continued. An elderly park keeper rescued us. He had a walking stick and waved the marauding youths away from us.

'You'll never get any thanks from the likes of them,' the old man said. He accompanied us all the way to the main square of the town, he protected us.

'They do the same thing to budgerigars,' he said as he turned to leave us.

'Yer what?' Colin and me chorused.

'Sparrers, sparrers, they always attack budgerigars. I suppose it's on account of them being different. You're like the budgerigars now, you've left the cage so you get pecked at a bit. Never mind, nobody will hurt yer now.' He sighed and walked away from us.

'If he had been the judge we would have won,' Colin said.

'We've got thirty bob each,' I wanted Colin to be happy again, his dejection was apparent even through the weird painted mask-like face.

'Get back in the pram; it's quicker if I push you.' It was an order, there was no way that I could console him. He never paused throughout that mile walk, sometimes he would stumble or sway over on one side because of the precarious design of his shoes, but he did not stop moving. I could see the burn marks on his clothing — his anger got us back home, back to the Star and Garter.

'Well, her mother must have been related to one of the judges darlin',' Ann Dando accepted our defeat as badly as Colin had done; she was referring to the winner of the competition. Comfort was needed more urgently in other quarters. Colin had removed his shoes. His feet were in an appalling mess. Blisters ballooned out from them and congealed blood covered most of the surface of the flesh. I looked at Ann whilst Colin stared down at his feet.

'You earned your money, Tommy, you earned it good and proper,' she spoke sadly.

It was 6.30, we sat in dressing gowns sipping gin and tonic. Colin's feet were immersed in a bowl of warm salted water.

'It'll be all right for you to stay over tonight Tommy?' Ann asked.

'Yes,' I said.

'You can both help out a bit behind the bar, but duck down if a policeman or the Salvation Army comes in. They wouldn't appreciate it. You feel better now our Colin?'

'Of course, of course I do,' he lied.

'That's politics for you,' Ann said.

'What?' I asked.

'Well, they change clothes to suit the scene — but you must always vote duck, you must always vote. If you don't vote then there might come a time when they won't give you a chance and that will be worse, Fancy Dress or not.' She left us. Colin patted his feet dry. Here and there they still oozed a little blood.

17

A Cigarette with Bette Davis

'I'll always love Dando. Don't ask me why, I don't know what I see in him. It will never come to anything, all we do is talk and laugh. If he kissed me, I don't know whether I would like it or not. I think that I'd probably die. Don't tell him I've told you this, I'll kill you if you do.' Margaret Slide said this to me more than once, she always used his surname when referring to him or when she was in his presence. Just like teachers at secondary schools do — it always sounded odd, after all she was his best friend and not his teacher.

'You know, of all the girls, Bomber Slide is the one. The one I want; I don't know how I want her. Do you think I might be in love with her? I can't be, can I? It's ridiculous, she's a mate but sometimes I think of her in other ways. I might be in love with her, but I don't dream about her and you're supposed to do that if you're in love. She's not special to look at, though not bad . . . . If you tell her what I've said you're for it. I'm warning you, don't tell her.' Colin Dando said things similar to this more than once. He called her 'Bomber' because he said that she could cause an explosion if she wanted to — I never understood the nick-name. I used it, and she never seemed to mind much.

I respected their confidential information about each other. Their affection or whatever it was remained like some undeclared treasure that never got past the customs officers. We went to lots of places together, I ought to have felt like a post-script or an addendum, knowing what I did about them. Yet they never gave me the impression that they did not want me there, sometimes I wondered if they were afraid of being alone together. Our weekly cinema visit was always an event. He would choose the film, that was why I was the first to arrive outside the Danilo.

The Danilo was the queen of cinemas, large, spacious, an enormous foyer and a balcony that Colin could not or would not resist whatever our joint economic circumstances might be. It was the biggest place of entertainment in Cannock, the only place that heralded its attractions with different coloured strip neon-lighting. I waited on the steps outside, 'Bette Davis' was written in electricity much larger than the title of the film. Colin was always the last to arrive, his excuses for being late varied from missing the bus to forgetting the time because he was playing the piano for his mother. Margaret and me never challenged or chided him. He never gave us time, he would speak as soon as he joined us.

'I couldn't find it anywhere, it had fallen behind the piano stool,' he was referring to a yellow woollen scarf that fell in correct proportions down his front and over his back.

'Yer don't play the piano wearing a scarf, do you? What have you got it on for now? It's not cold.' Margaret's observations were correct. I waited for the banter to finish. We had already missed some of the second feature because of his lateness.

'The trouble with you Bomber,' he gave his scarf another swing, 'the trouble with you is that you've got no imagination. If you had come tonight and not worn a frock, it would have been marvellous.'

126

She snorted and answered him as we mounted the cinema steps. 'I'd look a right bloody fool standing outside the pictures waiting for you in my underskirt. The whole of Cannock would look at me.'

'What could be better than that? We're going in the balcony Wakefield, have you got enough money?' I nodded. He motioned Margaret away from the sweet and popcorn kiosks.

'It's a Bette Davis film,' he whispered. 'I've got some cigarettes, you can't eat through her films. You have to smoke.' This edict worried me as I hated cigarette smoke, let alone smoking. I hoped that he would leave me out of the cigarette share-out.

'I've got ten Craven A,' he informed us. I climbed the stairs ahead of them. I called back and said that the 'little' film was nearly half over, and that we should hurry. This might help him forget about the cigarettes. He had the tickets and had no intention of being pushed up the stairs. He paused in the spacious lounge and sat down on one of the large sofas. He had kept the yellow scarf on, Margaret untwirled it from his neck and cast it into his lap. He made no comment on her action.

'Shall we have a fag now? There's three each, and one to pass along. We could smoke the odd one, just a few drags each.'

'Save them for inside,' said Margaret. We had to stand and wait for him because he had hung on to the tickets. As the usherette opened the door for us we heard a number of gunshots, a horse neighed.

'I hate cowboy films,' he said.

'There might be some Indians,' I added hopefully. Arrows always seemed more interesting than bullets, I always wanted the Indians to win but they rarely did. We took our seats and sat and talked through a mindless film which had something to do with cattle rustling. Somebody or other appeared to be cutting barbed wire fencing all the time and we had

127

come in at too late a stage to know who was good and who was bad. Colin said that the bad man was the one with the thin moustache, and that he would get shot in the end and that there was no point in thinking about it.

He was quite right. The film ended and 'The Cuckoo Waltz' was played on an organ as the usherettes paraded with their ice-cream trays. Three very tall men sat in front of us. They would have been quite within their rights to ask us to 'shut up talking' while the cowboy film was on. However, they had talked as well. Theirs was a foreign language — Polish, I think. They were left-overs from the War, these huge tall men who had chosen a twilight life in the coalmines of Staffordshire rather than return to their homelands. At the time, I couldn't understand this; I had asked my mother but she had shrugged and just said 'I suppose they think it's better here.' Ann Dando said that they stayed behind because they wanted to marry Cannock girls. She said that Cannock girls were prettier than anywhere else. I couldn't quarrel with this because I hadn't been to Poland. But I didn't accept it entirely; Indian girls in cowboy-and-Indian films always seemed to me to be pretty and they were quiet.

Gun shots opened the Bette Davis film and we were soon to see her in a postured state of distress. Her husband had been killed, they were living in a bungalow near the jungle. It was a posh bungalow and Bette was soon lighting a cigarette, pacing the lounge of her house, then sitting down, then getting up and puffing away at her fag. 'Oh marvellous, I like her better when she is going to be bad.' Colin had taken the cigarettes from his pocket. He passed one to Margaret who passed it along to me. Then she took one for herself. How did he know that Bette was going to be bad?

Colin and Margaret were inhaling and puffing out great clouds of smoke. I was having difficulty in lighting my cigarette as I could not bring myself to breathe in deeply enough to ignite it. The taste of the tobacco, even the smell of the brimstone when the match was struck, made me feel dizzy and sick. My nostrils as well as my mouth reacted violently to the proximity of the tobacco. I put my hand over the end of the cigarette and pretended it was alight. Occasionally, I would place it to my lips and improvise the action of my two friends. I would suck in my cheeks, throw my head back, and blow nothing into the ceiling except the nicotine-free air that still came from my lungs.

It was no good, I couldn't fool either of them for long. I don't know which of them detected my trickery first. Neither of them were going to let me get away with it. They were not derisive, nor cruel but sympathetic and imperative. Options like the one I had chosen simply would not do. I was not allowed to pretend, it had to be the real thing.

'Here, give him mine Bomber. It's already alight and pass his one back to me.' Margaret obeyed Colin and placed his lighted cigarette between my fingers. I held it awkwardly between my fingers as though it were alive, like the caress of a spider I could feel the smoke about my hands and face. Margaret was aware of my discomfort.

'It won't burn your fingers, it has a filter tip on it. You can stub it out before you reach the end of it.'

'Put it in your mouth like this,' Colin craned forward and I copied his action. I breathed in. It was worse than I had imagined; acrid, nasty tasting and a horrible sensation at the back of the throat. I coughed violently and let out the fumes as well as more spittle than I thought it possible to possess. Colin was a gentle teacher.

'Don't take in so much smoke, just little ones, little puffs. After a bit you can let it out through your mouth or through your nostrils.' He demonstrated both actions to perfection. The second time, he held his head back and threw a wonderful smoke ring up from his lips. The ring rose, wobbled and sailed over our heads before it finally dispersed. This skilful operation impressed me. In spite of my aversion I began inhaling minuscule amounts of smoke into my mouth and then puffed them out immediately. Colin and Margaret accepted this as valid. It was just as well, because I could not have coped with more during the first lesson.

Half way through the film and Bette was in dead trouble. All three of us were sure that she had murdered her husband. This was a wicked thing to do but no matter how bad she was we never wanted her to get caught. Colin said that if she was going to get caught it wouldn't be until the very end, because if she were caught there would be no film. Bomber said, 'You're so clever, Dando,' and he lit three more cigarettes to pass along the smoke barrier.

Somehow a quarter of my cigarette had managed to burn itself away and I had only had to put the thing to my mouth twice. Then I received a tap on the arm from Margaret, Colin had something to say to me.

'You have to flick it properly. Flick it like Bette.'

'Yer what?' I asked.

'The ash at the end of your fag,' said Margaret, pointing to the object I held between my fingers.

'Watch me, watch carefully, it's easy when you know how,' Colin said. He inhaled deeply, took the cigarette from his lips and then flicked the ash with his fore-finger. It all happened in one swift, smooth movement. The action was as impressive as the smoke ring had been. He began to do it a second time either because he was intent on being a thorough teacher or that he thought he was teaching a very stupid pupil. The second time he was swifter than the first. His over-confidence served him in poor fashion. What happened next caused Margaret and me to giggle and titter.

The cigarette spun from between his fingers and dropped behind the man who was sitting in front of Margaret. Colin did not laugh, he was nervous and exclaimed 'Oh! My God! Get it back Bomber, get it back. Lazlo will burn to death, his trousers, his suit . . . . '

Bomber began to laugh more, I wondered how Colin knew the man's name. A strong smell of burning cloth arose in the air. Margaret stopped laughing. We stubbed out our cigarettes.

I felt sick and Colin looked as if he were about to swoon. 'Excuse me, excuse me,' the man turned around to look at Margaret. He gazed directly into her face, the way some men did look at women. She understood his stare but ploughed on.

'Excuse me, would you mind standing up? Only I have my foot trapped in your seat,' she pointed to her foot which she had implanted under his seat. It wasn't stuck at all, but he smiled amiably and got up, and tilted his seat back. As he stood, Margaret bent over and flicked the burning ember away from the plush covering. He sat down again. Colin was still worried and agitated. We never saw the end of the film. 'We have to leave,' he whispered.

Some of the audience were surprised and annoyed that we left half-way through. We felt disappointed at missing out on Bette's destiny — but Margaret and me did not complain.

'That was an expensive suit he was wearing. All the Poles spend a lot of money on their clothes. Do you think I burned a hole in his trousers? I wonder if he'll recognise me if he sees me again. Do you think he will?'

'There's not much you can do about it if he does.' Bomber once more rescued us from tension, whether it was real or imaginary; there was a matter-of-factness about her that could always disperse anxiety.

She always accompanied us to our bus stops. She only lived a few hundred yards from the centre of the town, whereas both Colin and me lived in different outlying villages. We both caught different buses. If we had been gallant or chivalrous we ought to have seen her home first. She never expected this of us. Once when we had suggested it she had merely referred to our welfare saying that we might miss the last bus.

'Anyway, she shot her husband, I didn't want to tell you and spoil the picture, I saw it on Monday, I went with my mother to the afternoon showing . . . . ' he was full of surprises like this; he began to fill in some more details of the plot. It was as though he had been struck by

131

lightning. He clutched at his throat and suddenly stopped speaking.

I thought that the cigarettes were having some vile and terrible after effects upon him but Margaret could cope with his dramatics better than me.

'What's the matter now?' she asked dryly. She had already rescued him once.

'Me scarf, me yellow scarf, I've left it in the cinema, I can't go back in there and . . . . '

Margaret had already begun to journey back to the Danilo. 'Wait for me,' she called out over her shoulder.

'There's nobody like Bomber Slide,' his admiration for her always flooded when she was not around.

'Then tell her, tell her yourself,' I was angry but didn't know what I was angry about.

'If you say anything to her, if you say a word, I'll break your neck and I'll never see you again. Nor her, not ever — so remember that.' She returned with his scarf.

His bus drew in; he gave us garbled instructions to meet him on the Saturday for songs around the piano at his mother's pub. This meant him playing, him singing and us listening. We agreed to the arrangements and watched him leap on the bus platform. He looked down at us from the upstairs of the bus. With a certain amount of aplomb and grandeur he flung the scarf about his neck and then waved to us before the bus left.

'I don't know what I see in him,' she said.

'He has style,' I replied.

'Just like Bette Davis,' she added. 'My lipstick is called "Cyclamen", he bought it for me. Do you think I have too much on?'

'No, it looks all right to me.'

'Dando says I should make it heavier. I think he wants me to look like his mother,' she shrugged her shoulders and laughed and repeated the phrase, 'I don't know what I see in him, I don't.'

132

'Style, he's got style like Bette Davis,' I said.

She saw me to my bus. I crept on it and sat downstairs. Neither Colin or Margaret had ever asked me what I thought and felt about them. Perhaps this was a good thing because I would not have told them the truth.

18

Goodnight Kisses

There was no pain. All I could think of were the chestnuts, my bag had almost been full. The trees had lined the busy main road to Stafford. My cousin Ronnie had decided that it was time for us to leave for home. I remember my foot on the pedal of the bicycle . . . there was no pain.

A loud wailing noise that came from the ambulance brought the first of my senses back into focus. Then there was the smell and taste of my own blood as it seeped from my nose to my mouth. I wanted to spit out the taste, I opened my mouth. I made no other attempts to move. Even that slender movement was difficult, my jaws seemed sealed. Again I tried like some dumb goldfish. My lips parted and some blood and spittle trickled down my chin.

'Don't talk lad, no don't move. We'll soon have you free. Keep still now, don't upset yourself.' Even when the ambulance man spoke, when the white van came into view, when I saw the policeman doing things with tape measures, I felt that I was viewing something terrible rather than being a certain character in the happening.

'We could saw it off.'

One of my legs hurt, the other one I couldn't feel, I couldn't move it. Were they going to cut my leg off? Somehow, I looked down at what they were doing to the lower half of me.

My left leg, the one that did not hurt, was twisted at an odd angle. It was entangled with what was left of my bicycle. One of the brake handles had buried itself deeply in my calf. Two other men pulled at the mangled bicycle whilst the ambulance man held the leg. The pain came at this point, it was hot and fierce; it seemed to enter my whole body, not just my leg. Blood clouded my eyes, I tried to scream. It was less uncomfortable than a nightmare because at this point I slept. Consciousness left me and I was at peace.

'Oh, dear God, my pet, you've been here for two days now. You've been sleeping most of the time. That's what you needed to do — sleep. After a shock, sleep is very good and you had a bad shock my dear, very bad, you're lucky to be alive and here with us. Praise God.'

'Am I hurt very bad?' I knew that I had been in an accident and that I was in a hospital. I could smell the disinfectant and viewed my surroundings through one eye, the other had a bandage over it.

'To be sure, I've told you, you're lucky to be alive. I have to see to your face now.'

'Where am I hurt?'

'There's a cut over your left eye, but that's nicely stitched up, and you have broken your left leg, not a bad breakage, but you have a nasty cut on the leg.'

'Did you stitch that up? You're not going to take my leg off are you?'

'Dear God, darlin', no, we're not going to do anything like that. We have to let the wound heal, it's too wide to stitch. Don't worry my dear, don't worry, nature can be very kind. We'll get you well.' The nurse had begun to unwind the bandages from my head and face.

'This may hurt a little, my dear.' Her fingers were deft, they moved swiftly.

'You talk funny,' I said to her.

'I'm from Ireland, that's across the sea. It's on account of the sea crossing that our voices go up and down. Yes, up and down like the waves, now just keep still. I have to dress your face, I have to make you a handsome young man again. I will do that for you if you keep still my dear,' she had assembled a tray with lotions on it, and silver instruments, which I didn't like the look of.

'I like the way you talk,' I said.

'Do you my dear? Oh then my darlin' you can be my boy friend, but now you've got to keep still.'

'Haven't you got a boy friend? Ouch!'

'It will hurt a little but you have to be brave.' She was dabbing at my face, the cotton wool held firmly between the tweezers. She would dip the tweezers in the lotions and pick and dab at my face.

It was easier to keep talking, it took my mind off what she was doing. This was a painful and unpleasant process for me. She was very thorough, she worked at my face as though she were creating some marvellous piece of sculpture. She talked too, perhaps it helped her as well.

'No boy friends for me, you're my boy friend. I've told you.' I didn't believe her.

'You must have lots of them,' I had begun to appreciate her auburn hair and green eyes.

'Now where would you get an idea like that from? I would only have one boy friend at a time. I wouldn't go against the laws of God, my dear.' A small gold cross hung from her throat, I didn't know the laws on such matters but the nurse seemed to mean what she had said. My face had begun to sting. I winced and closed my right eye. Darkness, I couldn't see anything at all. I clutched at her arm, panic stricken.

'Have I lost one of my eyes?' She stroked the back of my hand.

'Tom, Tom, Tom, no you haven't. It's just bruised and

swollen, it's closed up for a time. It will be open tomorrow or the day after. That's what I'm doing here. Now, are you going to let me get you handsome again? I promise you I will, but you must be brave.' I let go of her wrist. She continued and I told her that she was Irish and she agreed that she was.

My hair was being brushed and the picking and dabbing ordeal was over for a time. Another nurse had joined the one who was tending me.

'How is he nurse?' The other nurse had a different uniform, and my nurse all but stood to attention when the question was asked of her.

'Oh, to be sure sister, he's with us now.' Where had I been before? Concussion was beyond my understanding.

'I would leave him free of the bandages. Dress the face three times a day for the first week. Doctor says the abrasions are superficial.'

'Oh, I'm sure they look worse than they are,' the nurse smiled at me. 'We'll soon have you looking good.'

'Can I see myself now?' I asked.

'Later, later,' said the sister and bustled away.

'Doesn't she know your name?' I asked.

'Yes darlin', but it's not done on wards, to be sure it's not. I'm nurse and she is sister.'

'What is your name?'

'It's Mary, but you must call me nurse.'

'All right, Nurse Mary.'

'None of your cheek Tommy, now I'll have no cheek from you.' Nevertheless, she laughed at my response.

She handed me a funny shaped bottle, it was twisted at the neck and had a long funnel.

'It's about time you used your water-works.'

'What?'

'Have a piddle,' she whispered.

I rejected the idea immediately, nobody would make me piss in a bottle. I did want to piddle but not in that thing.

I pushed the bottle back into her hands, she looked injured as though I had clouted her or something like that.

'Get me up, I can go to the lavatory,' I shouted at her, angry and shamed by her suggestion.

'My dear, you can't get up from this bed for at least three weeks. If you don't piddle, you will wet the bed. Shall I show you how to do it?' she had placed the bottle between my legs, and had already undone the top of my pyjamas. 'Now where's your Jimmy? You've got to place it carefully in the neck of the bottle.' She fumbled about, I was both alarmed and excited.

'I can do it, I can do it,' I cried. I positioned myself into the neck of the bottle. 'Can you go away for a bit nurse, then I can do it.' I'd already begun to half regret that I had not let her manoeuvre my 'Jimmy' for me. She left and I could hear the urine swishing as it spurted into the bottle. I was most careful, if any had gone on the sheets it would have meant that I had failed her. Faith in my healer was my guide and on my first attempt I achieved a direct hit, not a spot on the sheets. She returned and covered the bottle with a towel.

'You've done well, darlin',' she said.

I felt very proud, I would have pissed over the top of the hospital roof if she had wanted me to.

My parents were dutiful about visiting me. On the first visit, my mother sat by the side of the bed, looked at me and then began to cry. I couldn't ever remember her doing this before, the action both shocked and surprised me. We were ungiven to comforting one another and I felt incompetent lying there propped up in bed. I couldn't reach out to her.

'He's through the worst now Esther, it's no use getting yourself upset.' My father's words restrained her a little and she stopped weeping as abruptly as she had begun.

'But look at the state of him,' she said.

'He'll mend, the sister says he'll be unmarked. No blemishes on him, p'raps just a scar on his left eye or over it.'

'Do you hurt anywhere?' she asked me.

138

'No,' I replied truthfully and then began to chatter to them as if I were staying at some kind of holiday camp. They were very long days, those hospital days. Sleep was often difficult to achieve and no sooner than one had got to sleep it seemed that it was time to be woken up. We were aroused very early, I don't think I had ever been awake as early before. There were nurses who came around with bowls of water and face-flannels. They washed most of the other children, but only cleaned me under the armpits and on my hands. My face was now being powdered in the mornings and I could see through both eyes. I told my parents about these routines, but kept safe any information about Nurse Mary. I felt that this was private to me. I did not wish to share her with anyone.

'Can I see myself?' It was late afternoon and Nurse Mary was doing her dabbing and picking at my face. She did not answer me but gently brushed my hair. She was assembling her trolley — about to leave.

'I want a mirror, I want to have a look, if you don't let me have a mirror I won't let you touch me again. I'll fight and kick if you come near me.' I must have startled her, she had never heard me being wilful before. She did not answer me, but moved closer towards the bed and pulled up a stool. The green eyes clouded, but this did not deter me.

'I mean it, I mean it,' I spoke quietly, she accepted my determination and produced a hand mirror from the drawer.

'There,' she said, holding the mirror up for me to gaze into.

For some reason, I wasn't shocked, mainly because I couldn't accept the fact that the face that I was looking at was mine.

'They're drying up beautifully,' the nurse was referring to the huge scabs which covered seven-eighths of my face. The face that I looked at didn't seem at all beautiful to me; if it belonged to me, then I was resigned to the fact that I would remain permanently hideous. 'I'm ugly. I look like somebody from a horror film. I'm ugly, aren't I?' My questions were flat sounding and hopeless.

139

'Oh, don't talk such nonsense. I've never heard of such a thing.' It was as though she acted involuntarily, casting nursing rules aside. She bent towards me and a wisp of her hair tickled my ear, she kissed me full on the lips.

'I couldn't do that now could I? I couldn't do that if you were ugly.' She stood and looked about her on the ward. There were no witnesses, she patted my hand and trundled the trolley away. She left me feeling the clean smell of her and the taste of her mouth. She also left me with an erection that caused me some thrill and some discomfort. It seemed ages before it went away — almost painful, yet I was glad of it. From this time on, I was a model patient.

'Where were you? Why didn't you tell me that you were leaving?' It was late evening and Nurse Mary was tucking up my bed sheets.

'Since when did I have to report everything to you? I had two days off, now I am on night duty for a fortnight. This means that I see that everybody in the ward is comfortable and settled for the night and if anyone wants me, I am there. I have to sit up all through the night.'

'When do you sleep?'

'During the day, but I don't sleep so well in the day time, it's a bit unnatural but you get used to it after the first few days. Now are you settled? I want to put out your light.'

'Kiss me.' She pecked the top of my head. This was not what I was asking for.

'On the lips please?' I pleaded with her. She switched off the overhead lights and complied. This pattern she accepted as part of my cure, and it continued throughout her evening stints.

'You've not to tell anyone, but my first name is Theresa. Theresa Mary, those are my true names. I don't use Theresa because there are no other Theresas over here and it sounds unusual. There are lots in Ireland where I come from. She was a Saint.'

'Who?'

'Theresa — Saint Theresa, my name-sake.'

'What's a saint?'

'Surely to God you know what a saint is? Why it's true, they bring you up "Godless" over here. A saint is a good person who is with Our Lady in Heaven. We pray to saints to ask God for things and of course to forgive us any wickedness.'

'You're not wicked. I like the name Theresa. I like the sound of it, The-re-sa.' I had already told her that I loved her — but she had only laughed and said that I shouldn't think of such things. She wasn't to think of them because she had ever so many brothers and sisters in Ireland, she sent money home to her mother and father. I mentioned marriage.

'The man I marry will have to be good to me, or I won't marry at all. Not all men are good and I don't want to be blessed with a bad one.' How could she be blessed with a bad man? There were lots of things that she said that I didn't understand and she said that I would understand when I was older. I longed to be very old, at least twenty, then I could go away with Theresa and be good to her.

Long after she kissed me goodnight I would lie awake and look at her. She sat at a polished table which was placed in the middle of the ward. A small table lamp threw a pool of light about her features. The pale face, the wide brow, and the rich auburn hair underneath the strange cap took on enormous significance. As far as I was concerned, she had already achieved sanctity and seeing her lit up in this way, making notes, studying books, occasionally rising to minister to some child that called out, only served to intensify my love for her. I worshipped her from my bed; Theresa would not have thought this right as she often stated that she ought to be better than she was.

Towards the end of the month, I was walking and with the aid of some painful physiotherapy and Theresa's strictures that I 'must cooperate' with the rather hard ladies dressed in white who made me stand up straight and use my heel and toe, I began to walk with very little trace of a limp. I was sad that my condition had improved so rapidly. It meant that I saw less of Theresa. Constipation gave me an hour to myself with her. I ought to have felt awkward or ashamed when she inserted the rubber tube inside my behind. The rush of water swirling inside of me was a most curious sensation. She carefully poured the correct content down the funnel.

'Don't move or wriggle about,' she said. 'We'll soon clear you out.' As always, she was correct. Within minutes, perhaps seconds of the operation, she deftly slid the bed-pan under me. I exploded. The fart reverberated around the ward. I apologised to her, but she stood by me as I shat into the pan. I thought that I was never going to stop. She wiped my bottom and instead of recoiling from the mess and stench, she calmly recovered it from beneath me and covered it with a cloth. Then, she congratulated me, said that I had done well.

'Your bowels are clear now and it will help us all no end. A clearance is always good for you. It's only like unblocking a drain.' I watched her face as she took the stinking pan away. She might just as well have been carrying a tray of cosmetics. The contents of the pan did not seem to affect her.

My parents brought her some flowers and a box of chocolates. They had arrived to take me home. The ward was busy and there were many demands being made on Theresa. My bed was needed for a new urgent case. She was already beginning to change the sheets for its next inmate.

'Is it a boy?' I asked her.

'Yes my dear, poor child, he has been injured. Injured very badly, they're operating on him now,' she changed the pillow cases as she answered me.

'Are you the same with all of them?'

'What? What did you say my dear?' A wisp of hair had fallen on to her brow and she looked rushed and harassed.

'Do you . . . do you look after all the boys in the same way as you did me?'

'Of course she does,' my mother bundled my raincoat

on to me and looked at Theresa apologetically, half ashamed of her possessive son. Theresa paused for a fraction of a second and quickly kissed my forehead.

'I like all of them — but you were special. Yes, you were a bit different.'

'Say Ta-Ra then our Tom,' my father had taken my hand. I didn't say anything to Theresa, I waved my hand and walked away, my last glimpse of her was of her black-stockinged legs, she was bending over the bed putting the finishing touches to her role of comforter-in-command.

It was raining outside. We travelled on top of the bus. It was the same road where I had experienced my accident some weeks before. 'Here, here, it was just about here when the car hit you.' My father drew my attention to the window. It was bespattered with rain and I could only just make out the chestnut trees which lined the roadside. My view of them was blurred and unclear, I peered more intently and pressed my nose against the window. I remained like this long after we had passed the near fatal spot.

My father gently pulled me back into the seat. 'You'll bump your head travellin' like that.' I had wanted to hide my sobs from him. 'Don't cry lad, don't cry, it's all over now. We are going home. You'll soon be home,' he said. How could I tell them that . . . that I still needed to see her. I never did see her, not ever again.

19

Complete

The men manoeuvred the lorry-loads of coal with great care. Somehow, they managed to reverse the truck into the exact position. They used a hand winch to raise the chassis to an angle — when the chains lifted sufficiently, the back flap of the lorry was released and the coal was deposited just two yards from the coal house door. My mother and I watched this skilful operation. I stood near her, she looked at the great heap of coal and smiled sadly. 'There's a lot of slack in that coal, I'll have to use it for the boiler.'

She was calm and accepting about the delivery which was not up to standard. We relied on the coal for cooking, heating all of our water, and for warmth. If stocks got low my mother would worry. There were no frowns across her brow at this moment, I had never seen her so tranquil. I opened the coal house door, turned to her, and said 'I'll get it in for you mam.'

On normal occasions she would never allow me to do this, my father had constructed a wall made up of large pieces of coal and placed them at the front of the coal house. It was necessary to divide the larger pieces of coal from the smaller nuts and stack them behind the wall separately. The slack was left in a pile outside to keep the boiler going on Monday wash-days. I expected her to say no to my offer, but she nodded her head and took up the small pink jacket that she had almost completed knitting. The perm had gone from her hair, the soft curls suited her better, the long buttoned-up-the-middle flowered dress flowed almost down to her ankles. However, the special dress did not altogether disguise the bulge of her belly. She had stopped working and I had been informed that my parents had 'ordered' a baby from the hospital.

I knew where babies came from but not precisely how they managed to get out. I knew that my mother was carrying one, but if they chose to want me to believe that babies were ordered like a tin of pilchards, then I didn't have the effrontery to call them liars. I had expressed my pleasure about the forthcoming child.

'Is there a long waiting list?' I asked her.

'Oh, yes, there is, there always is — nearly a year you have to wait.'

'Jimmy said it was nine months.'

'Oh did he? Clever dick he is; how would he know? Leave the big pieces of coal or you'll hurt yourself. Your dad will get the big pieces in when he gets back from work.' She directed my attention away from the baby on to the task at hand.

'Change into your old clothes before you start.' I left her there in the sun with the knitting needles flashing swiftly this way and that.

A baby or the pending arrival of one, filled me with a strange excitement. I had a brother but he was so much older than myself. We never talked, never accompanied each other anywhere and rarely communicated at any level. My father had said we were as different as peas in a pod. This was true; if it were not for a physical resemblance then the neighbourhood would hardly have been aware that we existed in the same house. Adults or children never asked either of us any-thing about the other. We were related only by blood, same pod, but very different peas. We respected the differences and kept out of each other's way with no more animosity than is usual between brothers of a six-year age gap.

'Use the sieve our Tom.' I had got most of the coal housed but there was a pile of dust and small pieces left to one side. In her present state, my mother was much less abrasive in her manner, she delivered the instruction quietly and then chose not to watch me complete the job. After I had completed the work, she complimented me. Praise from her had in the past been difficult to come by, and I felt proud and satisfied. Usually she expressed dismay at any attempts that I made at doing things of a practical nature. I sat on the ground next to her, and leaned my head against her thigh. This was too much. 'Sit up, sit up properly, you'll cover my frock with coal dust.' I did as I was told, but remained sitting near her.

'I'll help look after it, mam,' I referred to her forthcoming baby. She carried on with her knitting, strangely removed from me, removed from all of us. Her pregnancy seemed to have placed her in a kind of dream world from which we were excluded.

'I'd like a sister, I can think of lots of girls' names,' I persisted.

'You'll have to take what comes along, although a little girl would be nice. Yes a little girl . . . . ' she got up from her chair, turned and pointed to it. I picked it up and followed her into the house.

'Now clean yourself up, wash your ears properly, you're covered with dust. When you've finished, off you go out to play. I don't want you under my heels. And don't get talking to everybody about the baby. It's nobody else's business.' I couldn't think why she wanted to be so secretive about it all, it was not an unusual occurrence. However, it seemed that for her it was particular and private, and that no one, not even her immediate family, should have much of a share in it.

When they took my mother away in an ambulance some two months later, I was surprised. Most of the other women in our street had borne their babies at home. I knew that I had been born in the house where I lived — not in a hospital.

'Yer mam is going to be in there for two or three weeks. I have to keep on working so you can stay with Mrs — she'll look after you during the day and give you yer dinner. I've arranged it all. I'm working the afternoon shifts, so I can't see to yer our Tom. It'll be all right again when yer mam comes out.' My father looked worried and haggard and I ceded to his plans without complaint. I would be able to see him in the late part of the morning. Not every morning, for there were hospital visits to be made.

After ten days or so, I received a yellow card from school. There were some mutterings from my class mates when the card was handed to me. I did not give the card to the kindly neighbour who was looking after me. She had three other children to see to, and in any event, the card was addressed to my parents. When I passed it to my father, he scowled. This was unusual for him, he stared at the card, he was a slow reader.

'Oh, if your mother knew about this she'd go bloody mad.' I wondered if I had done anything wrong. I scratched my head.

'We'd better get started straight away, we can't have you away from school,' he said.

I was bewildered and puzzled and looked at him questioningly. Initially, he chose not to enlighten me. He cleared the kitchen table and spread a newspaper on it. He placed the kettle over the fire and let it heat up. When the water was warm, he motioned me to follow him into the back kitchen and bent my head over the sink.

'I can wash my own hair,' I called out to him as the water ran into my eyes and trickled past my ears.

'Now this might sting a bit.' I could smell the Dettol. I think he ought to have diluted it more because my scalp

147

began to sting, he rinsed, rubbed and washed it, over and over again. I tried to move away from the sink, but he pulled me back. 'You've got bugs and nits in your head — got to get rid of all of them. If your mam comes back and finds you in this state there'll be all hell to pay.' He took me back into the kitchen, I bent my head over the newspaper and placed my hands behind my back. I was more interested in seeing the proof of my condition rather than being afraid of it, so I obediently leaned forward and craned my head over the newspaper. For some reason I tried to read the details of the paper. My father called it the 'scandal' paper. It arrived on Sundays and he always kept it out of my hands. At least, I had an opportunity of reading adult secrets.

I did not concentrate on the murders or rape for very long. I felt the fine tooth comb scraping at my scalp. He was very thorough, there was not a strand of hair that did not pass through the metal teeth of the comb. 'Crack them with your nails as they fall on to the paper. Be quick because they move fast.' I saw the first louse fall and was fascinated by its gruesome appearance and the progress it made across the print.

'Crack it, crack it with yer thumb nail.'

'Git it,' I crushed the creature before it reached the corner of the page. For the next twenty minutes I was busy cracking down on the lice as they fell from my head. I quite enjoyed it all. My father re-washed my hair once more and a fresh piece of newspaper was produced. The operation was repeated four or five times. At the end of the last of these sessions, no lice had plopped on to the page.

'I'm clear,' I said. I felt relieved about this, as my head felt sore and my neck had begun to ache.

'It's not over yet,' he said.

The torch which he took with him to the pit was produced. I was now requested to sit near the window, this position was a little more comfortable. The proceedings had now become irksome and boring. He shone the torch into my hair and then began picking and pulling at strands of hair. He showed me a tiny spear shaped white thing and then placed it between his thumb nails and crushed it. I heard it crack.

'They're the eggs; nits, that's what they are, nits. We have to get them all out or they'll hatch into lice in no time at all and you'll be back to where you started from, lousy.' He must have spent at least an hour on the nit-clearance routine. It required painstaking concentration on his part. He did not complain but occasionally he would shout in triumph, 'Git it!'

All this was repeated on the next two consecutive days; I had to report to the school clinic who declared me 'clear'. They congratulated me but I answered them that the honours were entirely due to my father's tenacity and concentration. He had been diligent about the home too — he cleaned and scrubbed it every day so that my mother could return to a house which was not in any kind of disorder.

'You'd better not tell yer mam about the lice, no need to worry her with that. You won't tell her, will you?'

'No,' I promised him.

She did not return to us by ambulance. I think a friend of my father who owned a car collected her and delivered her to us. I waited in the front room, anxious and excited. I saw the car draw up at the kerb side, my father sat in the back with my mother. He was holding something, my excitement increased and I scuttled down from the window and sat waiting for them to enter the kitchen. It was her suitcase that he was carrying, she held nothing. She sank down into an armchair, she neither looked nor spoke to me. My father brewed some tea and she accepted the cup as though she were hypnotised. She took a few sips of it before she spoke to him.

'All the clothes are in the side cupboard. There are napkins as well — they're all clean, all ready for wearing. You'd better take them down to Elsie, hers is due next month. Take them now.' He obeyed her and packed all the baby-clothing in two large carrier bags.

'Leave me on my own for a bit. Go on, take those things to Elsie, take them along with yer.' My father signalled me to join him. As we were leaving, she called out his name. 'Dick!' he paused at the kitchen doorway. I had entered the back kitchen ahead of him.

'Dick, Dick, she was all there you know — a little girl, lovely dark hair she had, but there wasn't an ounce of breath in her. They let me look at her — just once. No, there wasn't an ounce of breath in her.'

'Never mind Esther,' his reply seemed oddly inadequate.

'Aren't we having a baby, dad?' He did not answer me. I was almost having to run in order to keep up with him, he was walking very quickly. He delivered the clothes to Elsie and muttered something to her. 'Oh dear God,' the woman murmured, and thanked him for the clothing.

Clearly, he had decided on a long walk and I was not given a choice as to whether I should accompany him or not. He was not careful about crossing roads and on one occasion I had to restrain him from stepping underneath a bus. Eventually, we reached the canal and walked along the banks. A slight wind had risen and flecks of willow herb and dandelion seeds were blown into our faces. This was irritating as they tickled our nostrils and made us sneeze. This minor discomfort did not deter him from the walk. We paused when we reached the lock gates. He took up some pieces of shale and began to skim them across the water. Some of the shale bounced on the water two or three times before landing safely on the other side. I didn't join him in this activity, he seemed to be very angry and throwing the stones so that they bounced off the water and on to the other side of the bank seemed to help in some way. I began to feel cold, he was unaware of this and continued hurling the shale.

The arrival of a fisherman put a stop to this obsessive activity. I led him home, we took the same route. From time to time he would stop and shake his head and murmur, 'I don't know, I don't know.'

150

In spite of my father's remonstrations, my mother was back at work again within three weeks. She never referred to my sister ever again — neither did my father. It seemed unfair to me that after waiting so long . . . and the little girl had been all there.

20

Uniforms

'This letter says he has passed for the Grammar School.'

'Oh, ah, what's it say?'

'I've just told you what it says. He's passed for the Grammar School.' My parents discussed me and the letter as though I were not there. I glanced at the brown foolscap envelope. We didn't receive many letters, in fact the postman had to push all of our correspondence under the door because we had no letter box. I looked at the white typed piece of information, she looked to my father and chose to ignore my glance. She handed him the letter. He read more slowly than she did — yet he read more — she usually knitted or crocheted when she read. He placed the letter on the table before him. My mother showed no sense of pleasure as to the nature of its content. His face was not going to betray his feeling. He made a grunting noise from within his throat and then consulted me.

'Do you want to go?' I nodded. I had been rocketed into a secondary modern school before reaching the age of eleven. This was an expedient move on the part of the education authorities as primary schools were bulging at the seams. Men returning from the War seemed anxious to breed. I was not happy at the secondary modern school. All the teachers used canes and there was a great deal of emphasis on the practicalities of life. A whole day of woodwork and a half day spent doing 'rural science' in a ploughed field. I was not over-skilled in either. The letter constituted a release for me. I did not know to what I was going, except that I knew some travel would be involved and this prospect excited me. I looked at my father, who had said nothing after my affirmative.

'Well, that's it then, he goes,' he declared.

'Who's going to pay for it?' she asked.

'It says he's passed a scholarship, there's no money wanted for transport. He gets a pass for the bus and train. He won't have to pay for books.' He uttered a timid laugh. 'Them days are gone you know.' He smiled as he spoke but my mother's practicality remained insistent. She ran her finger down a list of items at the bottom of the letter as though she were scrutinising a shopping list.

'There's his uniform to be paid for, cap, blazer, two pair grey flannel trousers, sports things, a satchel, pocket money . . . ' she paused before she had completed her check list. 'And he'll be expected to stay at school longer, who's going to keep him? That's what I would like to know.'

'Me,' he said. She became irate.

'You say that now . . . . ' He stopped her, he held up his hand and showed his palm to signify a halt.

'I've said it, it's over, he wants to go, he's passed to go. And he's going.'

'Right then,' my mother gave her assent economically. The two words consolidated their agreement as to my future education. Her acceptance of our wishes was a grudging one. She punished him by sulking and answering any attempts that he made towards a conciliation by replying in a monosyllabic fashion. He bore all this stoically and busied himself with domestic chores. He insisted on washing up. I dried the crockery with the tea towel. My gratitude (if he was aware of it) was silent. So at the onset of adolescence my confusion was deepened. Yet inside me a kind of celebration took place. I was about to leave a school and a home environment the relevance of which I had already begun to question. I did not know exactly what I wanted, there were no high-flown or fanciful dreams — but escape, of one kind or another, did enter it all.

A new head teacher, a man called Gardiner, had instigated my transfer from all of this. He had placed two boys for this 'late entrance' examination six months after his arrival at the secondary modern school. We both passed. The other boy was to travel to Stafford Grammar School. This was a pity as Richard was a good friend of mine. Our new schools were miles apart. I don't think that we ever met again. Mr Gardiner was a benevolent man, a short time after he had been in the school, he had sent for me. I wondered if I had done something wrong.

It came as a surprise, he smiled and passed me a book. I glanced at the title, it was *Prester John* by John Buchan.

'You don't like gardening, do you Tom?' I shook my head.

'No sir, I don't.'

'Why? Some people find it very satisfying to grow things.'

'I can't keep my mind on it, it's boring, the afternoon always seems long. After a bit, I just feel that I want to do something else. My plot is one of the worst in the field sir, I know it is.'

He nodded, he was not the kind of man to tell a lie and invent prowess where it was not. 'Read. Read for me out loud. You can start at the first chapter.' The gardening did not seem to worry him and he was not angry with me for being disinterested in it.

'Mm-mm-mm, you certainly get your mouth around those long words, don't you? Do you read a lot? Tell me about some of the books that you have read.'

I extolled the virtues of Rider Haggard, Henty, Dickens

154

(and oddly enough, Frank Yerby). After this strange inter-
view, he gave me more time for reading and less gardening,
and showed that in a short space of time he was empathetic
to my needs. I was glad to be leaving his school, but I will
always remember him as a good, kind, sensitive man who had
noticed that I stuck out like a bramble-briar in the educa-
tional environment that was offered in the school at that
particular period. He had chosen to release me from it and
managed to let me know that his goodwill was travelling
with me. Comprehensive education whatever its future
warts or blessings, did not exist for us then. For children
like me, it was needed, but the key to its success ought to
have lain within the boundaries of its parochial appeal, rather
than its size. Either way, in spite of an assortment of affections for my village, my grammar school did offer an escape
route which I was glad to take. Throughout the August
holiday, I looked forward to the prospect of the new school
with both excitement and trepidation. September was
eventful in that it brought about a total change of social and
physical environment, and once more it brought me into
closer contact with my father.

Rising from my bed in the early dawn's semi-darkness
introduced me to a part of the day that had formerly been
unknown to me. The journey to my new school was awkward
rather than long. It required three modes of transport. It
was vital to catch the bus and the train, my father saw to it
that I did both. If one was late, the train was missed and so
was a day's schooling. So it happened that my father and I
got ready for our different destinations together before the
rest of the house. He always had the fire lit, and some tea and
toast ready for me before he got me out of bed.

We usually had fifteen minutes together before we left.
He would look me over, brush the red and gold blazer, see
that my grey flannels were unmarked, make sure that I put
my cap on (wearing the cap was a school rule). I couldn't
help but observe his appearance. His steel-capped boots,

his working trousers, his steel helmet and working gear, his cap — so different from mine. As a couple we must have looked incongruous. He was intent that I should look meticulous, he would polish my shoes and make the leather of the satchel shine. We left the house together, I was too occupied to be afraid. After a month the pattern was a settled one.

I was woken at five in the morning, and over breakfast he would show his interest in my welfare. He did not talk a lot, but what he said was much to the point.

'You done your homework, have you?'

'Yes Dad.'

'Oh ah, what did you do then?'

'Last night we had geography, English and Latin. I haven't finished the Latin. I'll do it on the train. It's just learning verbs. We have Latin every day, I don't see the point of it.'

'If they say you're to do it, then you do it. That's the point, it's simple our Tom. There's lots of things that I have to do that I don't see the point of — just get on with it. I don't know why they teach you Latin. Never heard anybody speak it. There must be a reason for it though, or they wouldn't teach it to you. What's a verb?'

'It's the word that does the "doing" in every sentence.' I knew he had not time to digest the meaning or understanding of my answer.

'Oh ah,' he would say. Then he would do a spot-check on us both.

'Got me snap, got me bottle of water Here's me spare laces — bag ready. Now you've got your satchel, see that you have the right books, here's your snap, there's an orange in the front room. Take one with you. Don't forget your bus pass and train pass.' He invested security in me in this way — daily without fail. His inventory of things to remember was his way of encouraging me for each new day. It never failed to work. I travelled with him on the 'pit bus' as far as Hednesford. The miners always greeted us, my school uniform left me strangely apart, the other passengers rarely spoke to me but nodded and smiled. I had the curious feeling that I was a bit in the way, and that they would all start talking when I got off the bus. It was then necessary for me to catch a steam train to Rugeley and from Rugeley Station there was a mile walk to the grammar school.

I cannot ever remember being late and absence was out of the question. Truancy would have been tantamount to enormous deceit, I could not ever deceive him. On the train journey, I had more time to spare, and in this way Latin or French verbs, the Tudors, the Synoptic Gospels all bit the dust. The journey gave me a study period bonus which I sorely needed.

The classes at school were streamed, i.e. Form 1A and Form 1B, Form 2A and Form 2B. This streaming continued throughout the school and the less able of what was then considered to be the *crême de la crême* of the populace were placed in a 'B' class. I found myself in Form 2B. The only way of moving from a 'B' class into an 'A' was to achieve a first, second or third in the examinations which were held every six months or so. It became imperative for me to compete, I had to get into an 'A' class. My parents would not have understood the significance of this, and I never explained why it was important. I had 'missed' a year and was forced to work very hard. The motivation was not self-induced, my father would not have liked it if I had let him know that the journey on the pit bus provided the main drive behind my studies.

I lied to the other boys on the train. When they moaned, and said that they had not done their homework, I did not wish to be labelled as a 'swot'. I said that I hadn't completed this work or read this chapter when, in fact, I had. After the first examination I managed to claw myself into second place in the form. I was praised by the head teacher during an assembly and informed that I would be moving into class IIIA. The 'A' status had been achieved, and selfishly I did not bother to enquire who was the unfortunate boy that I had displaced.

Feeling pleased, I gave my parents my first school report. In bold print on the right hand corner of the page it stated — 'Position in Class — second'. My mother spoke first.

'You let somebody beat you then?' I still suffer from the spear thrusts that she delivered in this strange, desultory fashion. I shrugged, the hurt must have reflected on my face. I chose not to answer her.

'Very good, very good, you can't win every time. Very good.' My father beamed and gave me half-a-crown. Later — perhaps two days later — he apologised for my mother's attitudes.

'She was pleased, yes she was very pleased really. Only she is not well. Not like she was when she was younger. No, she's not well at all, so don't let it chaff you when she says things like that. She doesn't mean it.' His observations were probably true, but at that time, bereft of his tolerance, I still found her manner towards him and me both wounding and unacceptable. The war years, the stresses and strains of only just coping with life over a period of time had left their indelible imprints on her. In the post war years, two major operations — one for a duodenal ulcer and another for a perforated ulcer — had finally left her drained and in a chronic state of nervous exhaustion and depression. My father accepted this legacy that she had been left with in stoical fashion, whilst I found it more difficult to stomach.

There were long days of silence from her, days when she raged without cause and days when she would sulk and withdraw from us. I found both facets, the silences and the nagging, equally difficult to contend with. Yet the anger, or whatever it was, I found more easily acceptable if it were directed towards me. When my father received the verbal arrows or spears, I would try to shield him and draw them on to me. Sometimes I succeeded. However, he always checked me for this, he did not wish for me to defend him. At times I found it impossible not to intervene, I could not understand that what I interpreted as tyranny he saw as illness. In

158

this he was right, I lacked his compassion and his innate understanding of the human condition.

My new status in an 'A' class made more demands on the family; there was virtually only one room available, this was shared by my mother, my father and me. Homework was set every night, it not only cut into my leisure, it affected theirs too.

'Grace Archer is dead. Burned to death, and I want to find out what's happened, so you can keep those books off the table. Don't start spreading them about.' This was my mother talking. I had cause to resent the particular radio-serial. I was always forced to give place to its broadcast and await my father's consent which coincided with him switching off the radio as the theme music heralded the never-ending saga of everyday country life.

'Right, it's over, you can start now.' He would clear the table for me. My mother would grunt, complain, sulk or knit or do a combination of all four. He read patiently or busied himself with domestic jobs elsewhere about the house. My mother's resentment with regard to the regime of enforced silence affected me and I found the atmosphere of the place unconducive for genuine study. I would read in bed, late into the night, always to hear my mother call out 'Don't forget to switch that light off before you go to sleep. We can't afford to burn money you know. All that bloody reading at this time is money burnt.' At this juncture of my life, I had not the pools of compassion that my father held in his reservoir. I disliked my mother.

My school uniform, with its maroon and gold colouring, came into focus as a future passport to escape from my environment. I felt like a cuckoo stuck in a strange nest, yet it was not in my make-up to kick anyone out of it. I began to spend a great deal of time away from home. Every other weekend I would stay with school friends in Rugeley so that my parents saw less and less of me. Even during the periods when I stayed at home, I distanced myself from them. I would spend a lot of time walking, a lot of time plotting out my future. All the plots and hopes were to take me away. My father must have sensed this, even at this very early stage of adolescence. 'Your hands are not made for coal-humping,' he would say. There was no point in trying to disagree with him. He let me take my walks alone.

My surroundings had changed, and there was a certain amount of regret when I re-visited former haunts of childhood mystery and excitement. Many of these places had begun to disappear. Housing estates stretched monotonously across land that had formerly been fields and meadows. Farms disappeared. Derelict jack pits and even larger mines were no longer left as monuments; they were flattened, the earth levelled. More houses and more people were absorbed. Small streams trickled to a halt in the face of this necessary progress and areas known as 'The Sunny Banks' were sunny no more. New friends were not to be found locally, my uniform saw to that.

I took up fishing once more, only to find that even the dark deep gravel pool had been pumped away. There seemed no doubt that the childhood I had known had gone forever. The tapestries of joy and distress were blanked out by the onset of adolescent confusion and aspiration.

In spite of the changes, the early years could not be castrated so easily, roots are not easily flung away. They return to me often — and still; they both worry and console me.

• DONA FLOR AND HER TWO HUSBANDS •
Jorge Amado

Dona Flor's first husband, a notorious gambler and woman-izer, has unexpectedly died. When the local pharmacist proposes to her, she accepts his hand in marriage. However, he is unable to satisfy her erotic visions. Then one night her first husband materializes at the foot of her bed . . .

'Jorge Amado has been writing immensely popular novels for fifty years. His books are on the grand scale, long, lavish, highly coloured, exuberant. . . . Amado has vigour, panache, raciness . . . a reputation as a master storyteller.' *TLS*

'a bacchanalia of a book: a veritable orgy of sex, food, gambling and mayhem' *CITY LIMITS*

576 pages   £6.95 (paper)

· FROM SLEEP UNBOUND ·
Andrée Chedid

Forced into a loveless arranged marriage at the age of fifteen, Samya feels a prisoner both of her husband and of traditional Arab society. Her dramatic act of revenge is both swift and liberatory. *From Sleep Unbound* is the first British publication of this prize winning novelist and poet.

'The slow dawning of the marriage's depths of humiliation, loneliness and sadness which crush her spirit and then paralyse her body is written so movingly that the sudden dramatic climax . . . comes as a relief of tension to the reader as to Samya. A brilliant, touching book . . .'
THE GUARDIAN

'Andrée Chedid manages to capture in the most eloquent style the flavour of Egypt. The hustle and bustle of the streets, the glory of the flame trees, the charm of the Nile . . . draw the reader into Samya's world . . . Beautifully translated.' *SPARE RIB*

'(*From Sleep Unbound*) is told rapidly and simply and the translation carefully emphasizes the sense of frustrated energy. A bitter comment on the experience of women.'
THE TIMES

160 pages £4.95 (paper)
The Sixth Day by Andrée Chedid is also available as a Serpent's Tail paperback.

• WINTER'S CHILD •
Dea Trier Mørch

Set in the maternity ward of a Copenhagen hospital, *Winter's Child* chronicles the elation and despair of eighteen women who each face a 'difficult' childbirth.

'You can almost smell the heavy perfume of birth, a mixture of blood and sweet milk. Evocative and powerful writing, it rings true to women's experience.' **SHEILA KITZINGER**

'communicates the very scent of birth' **VERNE MOBERG**

'simply wonderful' **CITY LIMITS**

'How I wish that *Winter's Child* had been written (when I was pregnant) . . . I came away from this book with a clearer perception of my own experience.' **WOMEN'S REVIEW**

Illustrated by the author
272 pages   £4.95 (paper)

· THE CHANEYSVILLE INCIDENT ·
David Bradley

The powerful story of John Washington's obsession with discovering the truth of what happened at Chaneysville and what it had to do with the deaths of his father and slave great-grandfather.

'an award-winning novel of the Black experience in the US' **THE BOOKSELLER**

'This is a very considerable novel indeed . . . (Bradley) can write a big scene in a way that any novelist might envy . . . the encounters between John (Washington) and his mother, and John and his father's executor are as fine and gripping and convincing as anything in Faulkner . . . an astonishing achievement' **THE SCOTSMAN**

'easily more sophisticated and exemplary than Ralph Ellison's *Invisible Man* . . . highly recommended' **CITY LIMITS**

'dazzling' **NEW STATESMAN**

WINNER OF THE AMERICAN PEN/FAULKNER PRIZE IN 1981

432 pages   £5.95 (paper)